THE BRICK MAN 3

Lock Down Publications and Ca$h
Presents
THE BRICK MAN 3
A Novel by *King Rio*

The Brick Man 3

Lock Down Publications
P.O. Box 944
Stockbridge, Ga 30281
www.lockdownpublications.com

Copyright 2021 by King Rio
The Brick Man 3

First Edition January 2022
Printed in the United States of America

This is a work of fiction. Names, characters, places, and incidents either are products of the author's imagination or are used fictitiously. Any similarity to actual events or locales or persons, living or dead, is entirely coincidental.

Lock Down Publications
Like our page on Facebook: Lock Down Publications @
www.facebook.com/lockdownpublications.ldp
Book interior design by: **Shawn Walker**

Stay Connected with Us!

Text **LOCKDOWN** to 22828 to stay up-to-date with new releases, sneak peaks, contests and more…

Thank you!

Submission Guideline.

Submit the first three chapters of your completed manuscript to ldpsubmissions@gmail.com, subject line: Your book's title. The manuscript must be in a .doc file and sent as an attachment. Document should be in Times New Roman, double spaced and in size 12 font. Also, provide your synopsis and full contact information. If sending multiple submissions, they must each be in a separate email.

Have a story but no way to send it electronically? You can still submit to LDP/Ca$h Presents. Send in the first three chapters, written or typed, of your completed manuscript to:

LDP: Submissions Dept
P.O. Box 944
Stockbridge, Ga 30281

DO NOT send original manuscript. Must be a duplicate.

Provide your synopsis and a cover letter containing your full contact information.

Thanks for considering LDP and Ca$h Presents.

King Rio

~Prologue~

December 20, 2016

"Go on," Blake said again. "Look in the bag."

They were in his penthouse apartment forty-five stories up. The carpet was deep cut and plush, as white as the snow piles outside. In the middle, between the desk chair where Blake sat and the genuine leather couch where no one at all sat, there was a brown shopping bag.

"If it's a payoff, forget it," Ashley Hunter said. "I love him…was too much to betray him."

"Who said anything about betrayal? It's money, but its not a payoff. Go ahead. Look." He was smoking a blunt of loud-smelling weed that was as big and round as a Cuban cigar. The air circulation system allowed her just a light whiff of the marijuana and then snatched it away. He was wearing a black and gold Versace robe on which a large gold letter B was embroidered. His eyes were calm and intelligent; the whites of them a bloody red from the weed he was inhaling. He looked just like what he was: a Grammy award winning, multi-platinum rap star who was unashamedly neck-deep in orga-nized crime.

She was in love with his biggest enemy and his biggest enemy was in love with her. She had expected him to make trouble and she knew this was it, but she just wasn't sure what type it was. She went to the shopping bag and tipped it over. Banded bundles of currency tumbled out onto the rug; all hundreds. She picked one of the bundles up and counted; twenty bills to a bundle. There were a lot of bundles.

"Two hundred thousand dollars," he said and then puffed

on his blunt.She looked at him. "And?"

"It's for you."

"I don't want it."

"You'll need it to bury your boyfriend... for real this time."

She didn't say anything. Her boyfriend had warned her how it would be. *He's like a snake*, she remembered him telling her. *An old rattlesnake full of venom. He'll try to make you a mouse.*

"So, you're engaged to an NBA player," he said. "Does Mr. Right know about your boyfriend?"

"Does it matter?"

"Oh, yes." He waved the blunt negligently. "It most definitely matters. You see, your Mr. Right is fairly new to the NBA. He's been signed to the Heat for all of four months. Word gets out that his bride-to-be is creeping with another man it could very likely break his spirit. Not to mention the damage it would do to your career. Right now, you're one of the most famous realityTV stars in the industry. They'll blackball you if this gets out."

"If you say so."

Blake smiled- a hundred grand worth of platinum and white diamonds encasing his choppers- and tilted back in the desk chair. He ran his thumb over the brass studs that held the black leather armrests to the ornate mahogany arms. "I invited you up because I thought we should have a little one-on-one chat, Ms. Hunter. Just a pleasant conversation between two civilized human beings, one of whom has a bit of information the other needs."

She started to reply but decided not to.

"Did you enjoy Vancouver?" Blake King asked, puffing lazily."Not particularly."

"I believe you spent time with a popular Canadian rapper

there. Half the night, if I'm correct."

"My boyfriend knows about it," she said and immediately wished she hadn't. She was playing his game, just what her boyfriend warned her against.

"They say we'll be getting up to eight inches by morning," he said, glancing out of the window at the far end of the room.

In the middle of the glass panes was a sliding glass door. Beyond it was a balcony the size of a cardboard box. Beyond that was a very long drop. There was something odd about the door. She couldn't quite put her finger on it.

"This is a very prestigious building," Blake said "Home to billionaires and Wall Street executives. When Salomon Brothers legend John Gutfreund died this past March he left this beautiful penthouse up for grabs. When I bought it it was the most expensive residential property on the market in all of New York City. A hundred and twenty million dollars. For that I get not only this nice twelve thousand square feet of living space, but also the very best security money can buy. Closed-circuit cameras and all that good stuff. When I knew you were in the lobby I made a phone call, had an employee of mine get into your car and plant a suicide note on your seat...typed of course. You couldn't keep lying to Mr. Right. He was a good man, the best thing that ever happened to you. You couldn't live with yourself. But, that sinner celebrity in you wanted to go out with a bang and who's more famous than me? Sure, you jump from my balcony and get your last fifteen minutes of fame. Genius, if you ask me."

He had thought it all out. She tried to cover herself as well as she could, but in the end she was child's play to him.

"You'll take that leap--that final, very nasty leap down onto Fifth Avenue--at exactly 11:45 unless you accept my offer."

"And all I have to do is tell you where he is?" Ashley

asked. "No deal, Blake. I don't know.

We set it up this way just for you."

"It's 11:07. You have time. Think it over.""Fuck you."

Blake sighed, leaned forward in his chair, and dropped the blunt into a chromium ashtray with a sliding lid. No fuss, no muss. The cigar-sized blunt and Ashley Hunter had been takencare of with equal ease. "You know," he said, "that son of yours is a handsome little fella. Reminds me of my own boys. I have three boys, one girl. Love them to death."

Her teeth came together in a tight clench. If not for the large black man who was standing behind her she might have launched herself at him. And now she knew what was wrong with the door in the middle of the glass. It was the middle of winter yet the screen had been taken off of the door and was leaning against the glass next to the door. Why would Blake have done that? But he'd already given her an idea as to why.

"Can you at least tell me *how* he did it?" Blake asked. "That's what I really, really want to know. That's what's been keeping me and my wife up these past few weeks."

"Haven't you ever heard of a body double? He found a guy who looked like him, had some surgery done to make the guy look even *more* like him, and had the guy take some voice-training lessons to sound like him. And there you have it. A perfect stranger became his identical twin. It was so convincing that not even I knew the difference between the two of them. I was actually with the body double when somebody shot him in the face and for a long time I thought my boyfriend was dead. I attended the wake and the funeral. I really had no idea that he was faking his death. Not until…"

"Until when?"

She shut down again. She had already said too much. The bull of a man behind her might assist her in committing an unwilling suicide if she told Blake everything he wanted to know. It was better to keep her lips sealed and let him do the talking. Her only job was to figure out how she was going to make it out of here alive--with or without the money.

There was a sound behind her; a footstep. She started to turn and something came down on the back of her head. There was no pain, but brilliant light seemed to leap across the room. Then,the room went dark.

~ ~ ~

When she woke up she was upside down forty-five stories in the air. The big man was holding her by the ankles. The back of her head was sending long, slow waves of pain toward the front of her head. She did a quarter of a sit-up expecting to find Blake standing next to the big man, but Blake was nowhere in sight. Instead, Blake's wife, the infamous Alexus Costilla, stood next to the big man in a full-length, white fur with her hands on her hips. The look Alexus had on her face was more like an evil Halloween mask than an angry expression.

Ashley's heart plunged down into her throat. A fine mist of snow assaulted her face. She fixed her mouth to scream, but Alexus leaned over the balcony and gave her an even meaner look.

"Scream," Alexus said. "Go head. Scream and see if I don't tell this man to drop your stupidass."

"Please," Ashley whimpered and looked down to the street far below.

The cars parked there were the size of those matchbox cars that kids played with back in the days. The ones driving by the building were just tiny pinpoints of light. Anyone falling that far would have plenty of time to realize just what was happening and to see the w ind blowing their clothes as the earth pulled them down faster and faster. You'd have time to scream a long, long scream and the sound you made when you hit the pavement would be like the sound of an overripe watermelon.

"Please?" Alexus echoed. "Did you say please? The only fucking thing that'll please me right now is if you tell me what I want to know. Now, either you tell me where he is or you drop.I'm done playing nice."

"He's in Jacksonville, Florida!" Ashley screamed. "T-Walk's in Jacksonville, Florida!"

~Chapter 1~

Across the street from Central Park Zoo sits 834 Fifth Avenue, a limestone sanctuary of Manhattan's elite for nearly a century. The top floor penthouse where the Kings -- Blake, Alexus, and their three children-- lived when they were in New York was a marble-ensconced, two-story apartment. Among its extravagances were 12.5 foot ceilings, a butler's pantry, a walk-

in safe, and walls adorned by meticulously preserved 17ᵗʰ century leather. Beyond the seven bedrooms and ten bathrooms lay a fifty foot-long living room made homey by two wood burningfireplaces.

After Brock, their Haitian bodyguard, had knocked Ashley unconscious, Blake had gone to the bathroom to spring a leak. By the time he returned, Brock was escorting Ashley out of the penthouse and Alexus was marching into their bedroom. He was seconds behind her.

"I know you didn't just let her go home!" Blake said.

Alexus put away her coat. Now she only wore a white t-shirt and white cotton short-shorts. "Bennett Creek Apartments in Jacksonville, Florida," she said and quickly climbed into the king- sized bed where she snuggled under the heavy white blanket. "God, it was so cold out there."

"So he's in Jacksonville? How do you know she's not ly-ing?" Blake disrobed and got into bed with her.

"She was telling the truth."

"But, she could've been lying. And how do you know she's not on the phone with him now telling him to get out of there?"

"Come on now, Blakey. Have faith in your wife. Do you think I'd truly just let her go home?Of course not. Enrique has some guys out front. They're gonna take her to that old warehouse I bought last year…the one I used to string up your old girlfriend when you couldn't keep your dick in your pants." She used an app on her iPhone 7 Plus that lowered the bedroom lights to a dim glow and then laid her head on his shoulder, gently scribbling on his chest with her fingernails. "Enrique's leaving for Florida immediately. We'll let the girl go once they have that apartment complex surrounded. She's lucky I've gotten out of the game…that I'm trying to do the right thing for our kids because I really wanted Brock to drop that hoe."

"I can't believe he's still alive.""Me neither."

"Can't you get arrested for faking your death?"

"I believe so." Alexus was on her iPhone again. She turned the heat up to 88 degrees and then made the television that was built into the mahogany table at the foot of their bed rise up from its hidden slot. "It doesn't matter anyway. He'll be dead before the cops even know he wasstill living."

Blake nodded. Maybe wifey was right. Maybe Trintino "T-Walk" Walkson would be dead by sunrise. In Blake's opinion that was a huge maybe. If T-Walk had somehow been able to make everyone think he was dead for this long there was no way he was going to be a sitting duck when the Costilla Cartel's henchmen showed up at the apartment complex where he was supposedly hiding out. No, T-Walk was way too cunning to fall for that.

"It won't work," Blake said. "He won't be there. I guarantee it.""So what do you suggest we do if he's not there?"

"Let Ashley go and keep track of her. Put one of those tracking devices on her car. She'll eventually lead us to him."

After all, it had been Ashley who'd alerted them to T-Walk being alive and well in the first place.

"We'll go over it all in the--" Alexus yawned, "--in the morning. I'm too sleepy to be discussing anything right now."

Alexus turned on a movie and Blake didn't ask what it was. A minute later he found out thatit was *Queen of Katwe*, starring the chocolate-hued African beauty Lupita Nyong'o. Blake glanced around the huge master bedroom, which their maids kept eerily neat, and thanked God for the blessing. Here he was, a 24-year-old black man who'd risen from rags to obscene riches, lying in bed next to the baddest chick he'd ever laid eyes on. He was the CEO of Money Bagz Management, the most successful black-owned record label in the music industry. He was Bulletface, the billionaire gangsta rap artist whose last studio album had sold ten million copies within ninety days of its release. He was the the father of three bad-ass kids: Savaria, 9; King, 5; Juan, 1. Yes, he was truly blessed beyond belief and he was grateful for the blessings.

"We have to go back to Africa one of these days," Alexus said dreamily. She returned her iPhone to the table on her side of the bed and was back on his shoulder watching the movie. "Not this month, but soon. This time we can bring the kids, show them where our ancestors camefrom."

"You mean *my* ancestors."

"I'm half black, thank you very much.""You' re Mexican."

"And black."

"This much." He held up his hand with his thumb and forefinger separated by half a centimeter. "So basically you're just a Mexican."

"Shhh. Watch the movie.""You wanna be black?"

She chuckled and shushed him again.

"You wanna join my African tribe?" he asked her.

"I'm not listening to you," Alexus said. The corners of her mouth curved up in a small but undeniably amused smile. "Leave me alone, Blake."

He moved on top of her, inhaling the sweet scent of her expensive perfume, and kissed her full, juicy lips. "You know

I got that Mandingo in my bloodline, right? I come from a long lineof Mandingo warriors."

Her smile widened a millimeter or two. "More like a long line of assholes. Can you move soI can watch this movie?"

"Mandingo warriors don't watch movies. We *make* movies.""Well, go and --"

Blake clamped a hand down over his wife's mouth and with his other hand he crept under her shirt and went from breast to breast, squeezing the soft globes and caressing the nipples. "Mandingo women only talk when spoken to with question. I no ask question." He took his handoff of her mouth and replaced it with his lips. The silencing hand then slipped its way down into her short-shorts. "Mandingo warrior fuck shit out of Mexican woman."

She laughed briefly at the African accent. Her body trembled beneath his. His probing handsand delicate kisses elicited a moan from deep within her. Her hand went in his boxer shorts and came out with his foot-long erection.

To a high man with the munchies there is perhaps nothing in the world more delicious than the taste of his woman's pussy. Blake was hungry for it. So hungry, in fact, that he skipped over the trail of kisses he usually planted on his way down to it. He peeled the short-shorts off and vacuum-sealed his lips around her clitoris. He pushed his middle finger into her all the way up tothe third knuckle and pressed up against her g-spot. She squirmed and moaned while graspingthe back of his head in both of her hands.

"Mmmm. Fuck! Yes. Mmmm....yeah," Alexus said, urgently humping his face.

He looked up at her, stared into those sexy green eyes of hers, and kept sucking until she tensed and fidgeted in orgasm. Her juices were his reward; he greedily lapped it all up.

"Oooh, Mandingo!" Alexus said and then tucked her lower

lip between her teeth. "I can get used to this."

Grinning wickedly, Blake stood up over her and pounded his fits on his heavily-muscled chest. He had been doing a lot of physical training lately in preparation for an upcoming movie role and it showed. His muscles were thick rolling slabs of concrete beneath his skin.

"Mandingo warrior!" he called out. "Here to put wet-ness on back of Mexican woman.

Wetback!" He tried to hold the laugh but it came out any-way.

She squinted at him. "Don't get this new identity of yours fucked up," she said with a smirk.

Anxious to feel her touch, he gripped the sides of his boxer shorts and practically ripped them off. They fell to the bed and he kicked the across the room.

Moving to her knees in front of him, Alexus reached out and sheathed him with her palms. His long black pole immediately thickened and pulsed with desire. The feel of her warm, soft fingers closing over his dick drove every sane thought from him.

Holding him in her hands, she opened her mouth and brushed her pretty pink tongue over her bottom lip. "I can't believe it's been six years since I first saw this thing and I still can't get over how bit it is."

She began kissing a path along the sides of his perilously long love muscle and the feel of her lips nearly took him over the edge. Blood pounded through his dick and he felt it grow another inch. He needed to touch her--to penetrate her, again and again. He reached down, stroked her breast, and pinched her hard nipple. She gasped and arched into him. Her uninhib-itedresponse brought him to new heights of arousal.

She looked up at him and lifted one perfect eyebrow. Her lips were parted and her waist-length hair, as straight as a razor's edge, was parted down the middle and hung down her back like Count Dracula's cape. Her warm breath fanned his engorged dick. She ran her tongue along her top lip and then it snaked out and licked a path along the length of him. He became lost in thesensation as his dick absorbed the warmth of her mouth.

Reaching down underneath him, she grasped his heavy sac. Gently cupping his balls, she gave a light squeeze. The erotic, silky sweep of her long black hair over his thighs sent him teetering on the edge.

He threw his head back and growled. "Damn," he cried out and knew that the couldn't take much more.

A drop of sweat trickled down his forehead as a tremor ripped through him. He gave a manly groan and fought to hang on. He wanted to lay her down to make love to her properly-- slowly, passionately, all night long. But, he knew he was well past the point of no return.

The tantalizing brush of her tongue as she licked the sensitive underside of his bulbous head may have brought him to the edge, but it was the firm grip of her hand pumping up and down hislength that tipped him over. He tangled his fingers in her hair when he felt the pressure of an approaching orgasm.

"Here it comes, baby!" He tugged her head to urge her back, but she didn't budge.

She kept her mouth wrapped around him and sucked long and hard. His breath came in a ragged burst and his whole body stilled with the blinding pleasure.

Muscles straining, he shouted his release-- a release so powerful and intense that his vision went fuzzy around the edges. It took him a moment to recapture his breath and regain his bearings. He looked down and smiled at his amazing woman. She was still jerking him though now her hand was moving slower, it's grip tighter to coax out the last drops of cum which she eagerly licked up and swallowed.

Alexus got out of bed and retrieved their underwear with her big butt bouncing with every step she took. "You better be up early so we can get you out of here before my husband gets here," she said with a beaming smile. "I'm sure Blake will throw a fit if he finds out I've cheatedon him with a Mandingo warrior."

"Yes. Must leave before Blake return. Mandingo warrior no match for real street nigga."She laughed. "You're so stupid."

"I was smart until I met you," he shot back.

"You had a rusty old Chevy Caprice when you met me. Couldn't have been too damnsmart." She climbed on the bed and they slipped beneath the covers. "Let's not forget how fat you were too."

"Why you bringing up old shit?"

Alexus went silent for a moment. She used her iPhone to lower the temperature by ten degrees down to seventy-eight (as Blake thanked God again) and then turned off the lights. Afterwards, she laid with her head on is chest and sighed. "I know you're probably tired of hearing me say this," she said, "but, Enrique's really been pressing me about the whole Chicago ordeal. He knows there's a ton of money to be made there. We need another guy like Cup, someone we can dump a few kilos on every month. *At least* a few hundred. You and I both knowfrom past experiences that the streets of Chicago are a gold mine."

"Well, if you hadn't kidnapped Bubbles and scared her half to death she'd probably be a lot more helpful to us with this matter."

"You shouldn't have been fucking her." "That's more old shit," Blake pointed out."Don't be a smart ass."

"I'm just saying, baby. Every time I call that girl's phone she ignores it. I'm not about to bea dumb ass and send a text saying what I want her to help me do."

"I don't see why you need her anyway."

"I need her because she's a stripper. She mingles with all the dope boys. She's the only person I know in Chicago…well, the only one I can trust who has that kind of access to the big dope boys. I was hoping to get a chance to talk to her when we went to Cup's old club a few months ago, but she left as soon as she saw you."

Her brow wrinkled. "Don't blame it on me. I was sitting at our table in VIP minding my own business and having a drink."

"It was your fault she left."

"No, it wasn't. And forget her anyway. Why can't we just go through Cup's son? I'm sure he's deep enough into the streets to know how to unload a few shipments every month or so." She tilted her head back and looked Blake in the eyes. "Be honest. You don't want to use him because of the situation you had with Cup. Am I wrong? You're still holding a grudge."

Blake didn't say anything. His eyes were on the movie, but his mind was on the memory of his daughter's mother. Her name was Ashley Joy and she had been murdered. Although Blake wasn't sure who the killer was, he did know for certain that Cup was ultimately responsible for her death. He knew this because the ransom money Alexus had helped him pay for Ashley and Savaria's safe return was eventually traced back to Cup and several other members of Cup's gang.

Ashley Joy was just one name on a list of people that Blake had lost since he'd started dating Alexus Costilla, the Texas-born beauty who had inherited a lucrative cable television network and a near fifty billion dollar fortune from her paternal grandmother. Not to mention a Mexican drug cartel; not just some random start-up drug cartel either. The Costilla Cartel had only recently lost its spot as Mexico's number one drug cartel. Now the Sinaloa Cartel was leading the race, followed closely by the Costilla and the Zeta cartels. Enrique, the man who'd once been Alexus's head of security, was now in charge of the Costilla Cartel's operations and he answered only to Alexus.

"I'll get on top of that in the morning," Blake said. "First thing."

"Good." Alexus shut her eyes. "Maybe Chicago will put us back in first place."

King Rio

~Chapter 2~

Wednesday, December 21, 2016

They had been predicting a blizzard all week and on Wednesday Chicago got it. A real snowstorm that piled up eight inches by four in the morning and showed no signs of slowing down. Lee Wilkins, alias Juice, had gotten up at the crack of dawn to fix breakfast for five: beef sausages scrambled eggs, hash browns, and toast. His girlfriend, Lakita Thomas, alias Bubbles, and her 12-year-old daughter had stayed over the previous night and his twin daughters who lived upstairs on the second floor would more than likely want plates too.

Juice was a big man, over sixty feet tall and over two hundred and forty pounds. He was bald-headed with a beer belly and a safe full of drug money. He was the laid back leader of a faction of Traveler Vice Lords in the North Lawndale neighborhood.

Ra'Mya, Lakita's daughter, came stumbling into the kitchen at six o'clock on the dot. "Mama's woke," she said and plopped down in a chair. She fingered crust out of the corners of her eyes and yawned for eight seconds. "Didn't know bald-headed people could cook. Smells good."

"You must be in the mood to make some snow angels this morning," Juice said, buttering a slice of toast.

"I suppose it is more sanitary," Ra'Mya mused. "Won't have to worry about any hair in the food. Bald-headed chefs might be the net big thing. You never know, step-dad."

"Ever seen a kid's bones break?"

"Are you threatening a twelve-year-old girl?"

"Is a twelve-year-old girl calling me a bald-headed chef?"

"Ma! Your boyfriend is in here threatening to break my

bones!""You lil' snitch." Juice chuckled.

"Juice!" Lakita shouted. "You better leave my baby alone!"

Ra'Mya gave a winning grin as Juice handed her a plate and a glass of cold milk. The two of them shared a laugh. He and Ra'Mya were always joking around. She was a smart kid, an honor roll student, and a soccer player. She also played basketball and she loved math. She had been quiet around Juice when he first started dating her mom, but in the four months since then she'd finally started opening up to him. On Thanksgiving she'd thanked him for loving her and her mom unconditionally. On the sixteenth of September he'd accompanied her to the father- daughter dance at her school in Lake Forest, Illinois. On Black Friday, he'd squandered more than five thousand dollars on Christmas gifts for her, all of which were now piled around the treein his living room.

Juice made two more plates--one for Lakita, the other for himself-- and then joined Ra'Mya at the dining room table. Lakita came out of the bathroom a minute later and they all began toeat, each of them thumbing through their iPhones with one hand while shoveling food in their mouths with the other.

"Oh God," Lakita said. Juice looked at her. "What?""He's calling me again."

Juice dropped his fork and it clattered loudly onto his plate. He clenched his teeth and flared his nostrils. "Want me to answer it?" he asked.

She shook her hand no. "I'll just ignore it like I usually do. He'll stop calling one of these days."

It was Juice's turn to shake his head. "Nah. Either you answer it and tell him to stop calling you or let me do it. He's stalking you. That's some weirdo shit. I could care less how much money the nigga got."

Juice was well aware of Lakita's past relationship with the rapper. While in prison he'd seen an episode of TMZ where they talked about her break-up with Bulletface as well as her alleged affair with one other rap legend. He'd seen her spreads in all of the magazines that featured predominantly African American women with Coke bottle curves and pretty faces He'd taped some of those pages on the wall in his cell and told his cellmates that he was going to get his money right when he got out and then head straight over to Redbone's Gentlemen's Club on the 1600 block of Trumbull Avenue to meet Bubbles, the brown-skinned woman King Magazine had named "the baddest stripper in all of Chicago".

With that being said, it was understandable why a big rap star like Bulletface would be hounding a woman like Lakita "Bubbles" Thomas. True enough, Bulletface had the baddest chick in the country; a woman with brains, beauty, booty, and bank. But, to a man with fame and an insane fortune in his favor, one woman was rarely enough. What Juice didn't understand was why Bulletface was still stuck on calling Lakita's phone when he had not only a wife but also a fan-base that consisted of tens of millions of women all across the world. The idea that Lakita might have something to do with it crossed Juice's mind. Maybe she was talking to Bulletface behind his back, ignoring the calls when he was present to keep the cat in the bag. His suspicions were put to rest two seconds later when she answered the call and put it on speakerphone.

"How many times do I have to send you to voice mail for you to get it through your skull that I'm not fucking with you?" she spoke into the phone. "Christ, you've been calling me all year and not once have I answered. You don't know what that means? Want me to spell it out for you?"

"I need your help with something. That's the only reason I'm calling. Damn, after all the shit I've done for you are you telling me I can't call and ask for your help?"

Now Ra'Mya dropped her fork. "Oh my God!" she whispered quickly. "That's Bulletface! That's actually Bulletface!" She began to fan her face with both hands as her eyeballs rolled around in her head like ball bearings.

Juice and Bubbles stared at each other. "What kind of help?" Bubbles asked finally.

"I just need you to point me in the right direction," the rap god said. "What's that mean?"

"I can't talk about it on the phone, but we'll be in Malibu later this week. Think you canmeet me there?"

"Malibu? You mean Malibu as in Malibu, California?"

"That's the one. I'll wire you a hundred grand for any inconvenience this might cause. You'll be back home before Christmas." Before she had time to reply, Blake "Bulletface" King said, "And please don't think I'm trying to…you know…because that's not the case at all. My wife and I are in a good place. This is business. That's it, that's all."

"Good because my boyfriend and I are also in a good place."

"Is that the guy who was with you at The Visionary Lounge back in September?"

Bubbles read the uncertainty in Juice's eyes and replied accordingly. "Does it matter?" sheasked, sighing.

"It might. Is he a street nigga?"

"Of course. What kind of question is that? You know I ain't fuckin' with no *square* nigga."Blake paused.

Leaning forward in her seat, Ra'Mya was all ears.

Juice forked a pile of scrambled eggs in his mouth and took a bite of his toasted bread. "Okay," the rapper said finally. "You remember the relationship I had with Cup? The

business relationship. That's what I need. I need somebody like Cup."

"My boyfriend was actually Cup's best friend. He was in prison when you and Cup were inbusiness together."

"Bring him with you. Let him know it'll be worth the trip."

If life was a cartoon, Juice's eyes would have spun like the wheels in a slot machine and landed on shimmering gold dollar signs.

King Rio

~Chapter 3~

It was half past seven in the morning according to the watch on her wrist when Kenya Nelson heard her cell phone ring. She knew without even looking at it that it was him. It was her ex. The reason she was lying on Dr. Farr's couch in the first place. She dug the smart phone out of her pocket, adjusted it to silent, and then tucked it back in her jeans.

"I came to you because I want to tell somebody about this before it's splashed all over the news tomorrow morning," Kenya said. "I can't go to a priest because I'm not Catholic. I've thought of going to a lawyer but I don't believe I've done anything to consult a lawyer about." She took a moment to think a bout it. "All I did was take him in."

Dr. Farr turned on the tape recorder.

Kenya lay straight as a ruler on the white lather couch in Dr. Melonie Farr's downtown Los Angeles office. Her feet protruded stiffly over the couch's end; the picture of a woman enduring necessary humiliation. Her hands were folded corpse-like on her chest. Her face was carefully set. She looked at the plain white stucco ceiling as if seeing scenes and pictures played out there.

"You took him in?" Dr. Farr repeated. "Who did you take--"

"Wait." Kenya gave an impatient flick of her hand. "He showed up at my place in the middle of the night. This was January of last year, a week or tow before I left the WNBA for good. I was dead sleep when my doorbell rang. I went and answered the door and there he was."

Dr. Farr said nothing. She thought that Kenya looked para-noid and bone-tired. Her dark skinwas dry and her ponytail was disheveled. Her eyes held all the miserable secrets of cognac.

"They were after him," Kenya went on. "But no one would have believed that. Not even after what happened to Demarko Rumsfeld. Nobody would've believed it. If they would have, things would be alright."

"Why is that?""Because…"

Kenya broke off and darted up on her elbows, staring across the room. "What's that?" she barked. Her eyes had narrowed to stringent slits.

"What's what?"

"That noise outside the door."

"My secretary," Dr. Farr said. "Probably just getting in." "Open it. I want to see."

Dr. Farr got up wordlessly, crossed the room, and opened the door. Julie, her secretary, was sitting at the desk with a cup of Starbucks in one hand and an iPhone in the other. That was all.

"Alright?" Dr. Farr asked.

"Alright." Kenya removed the props of her elbows and returned to her previous position. "You were saying," Dr. Farr said as she went back to her chair, "that if the fact that they were after him could be proved, all your troubles would be over. Why is that?"

"He'd be free," Kenya said immediately. "Free to do whatever t he hell it is he wants to do.

Free to leave me the hell alone." She smiled at nothing. "Who is this person they were after?"

"Don't try to snatch it out of me!" Kenya jerked around and stared balefully at Farr. "I'll tell you, don't worry. I'm not one of your nut jobs bouncing around and pretending to be Elvis or explaining that I got hooked on heroin because my father didn't love me. I know you won't believe me. I don't care. It doesn't matter. Just to talk about it will be enough."

"Alright." Dr. Farr nodded skeptically.

"I met him in 2011. I was nineteen and he was twenty-four. My cousin was his girlfriend. She was pregnant." Her lips twisted in a sneaky, cold grin that was gone in a wink. "I was in college and it wasn't easy making time for the two of us when we first started hooking up, but I didn't mind. I loved him. We were happy together. And the dick was good, so I was hooked.

"Then he started fucking some reality TV whore with fake ass for days. I tried to look past that, tried to love that dog-ass nigga through all the bullshit. But, I couldn't just keep letting him cheat on me like that. Don't you just hate bitches with fake butts?"

Farr grunted noncommittally.

"It doesn't matter, though. I loved him anyway." She said it almost vengefully as if she had loved the guy to spite the side chick.

"Who is he?" Far asked.

"T-Walk," Kenya Nelson answered immediately. "T-Walk ain't dead at all. Just been hidingout with me since his funeral." She twisted around and grinned. "You think I'm crazy alright. It'swritten all over your face. But I don't care. All I want to do is tell you and then get lost."

"I'm listening," Farr said.

"It started when he fell out with Blake over my cousin Alexus. Now see, T-Walk had alwaysbeen a gang member--a Gangster Disciple if I'm not mistaken-- so beef was nothing new to him. We had a condo in Chicago back then and he literally had guns in every room. At first he thoughthe would win the war with Blake. I mean, T-Walk already had six figures and a nightclub when he first got with Alexus, and Blake was really a nobody at the time. So, when the shit kicked off he sent three of his guys, K.G, Craig, and my brother Bookie, at Blake. Blake ended up shooting all three of them and killing K.G. and they shot Blake a bunch of times. Two of the bullets went through one jaw and out the other. That's how he got the rap name 'Bulletface'.

"After a while though, when the beef began to seem like it would never end, T-Walk started to worry. Blake healed up and came back with a fuckin' vengeance. Not only did he shoot T-Walk on two different occasions, but he also killed Craig and my brother Bookie. There were a lot of other murders...T-Walk lost a lot of friends. It was a scary time for him. He started wearing body armor, bullet-proofing his cars, looking over his shoulder everywhere he went, especially after Alexus's grandma died and left her all that money. Because you see, Alexus was kind of like that girl in the *Twilight* movies-- torn between vampire and werewolf. Her family wanted her to be with T-Walk because he was a business-first kinda man, but she was crazy in love with Blake. That meant her power was his and he used it to strike at T-Walk's gang. That's what really worried T-Walk, what made him go to such lengths to protect himself from being thenext dead body.

"He set his plan in motion slowly after he became a TV producer. That's when Brick House reality TV franchise made him a huge celebrity in Hollywood, so nobody suspected a thing whenhe had a casting call for an autobiographical film that would supposedly detail his rise to success.The casting call was done in seventeen states over the span of five or six months. He was searching for someone who looked so much like him that people would think they guy *was* him. He found what he was looking for in Demarko Rumsfeld, a college student from Jackson, Mississippi. He paid Rumsfeld a million dollars to become his body double, promising another million every year. Rumsfeld accepted the offer and the second T-Walk was born.

"Rumsfeld had his name legally changed to Trintino Walkson. He had a mole removed from his neck, got all the tattoos that the real T-Walk had, and underwent a minor lip reduction surgery. He listened to hours of recordings again and again to learn how to talk like the real T-Walk. The whole nine. He even took the real T-Walk's girlfriend-- the bitch with the fake ass from that Brick House show...Ashley Hunter, but they called her Thunder on the show. He took her out on dates and everything and she actually thought it was T-Walk. Rumsfeld was with her in south Florida when a sniper took him out."

"Did you know it was the fake T-Walk then?" Farr asked softly.

"Oh, no. Not then. But I did see one thing. It didn't mean anything to me then, but my mind stored it away."

"What was that?"

"The real T-Walk's left ear was missing part of the lobe from when Blake shot him the second time. I used to joke with him about it. The body in the casket at the funeral had a perfect left ear."

"Okay. What happened then?"

Kenya shrugged. "We buried him." She looked morbidly at her hands as if she had done the burying herself.

"And the next thing you know he's at your front door?"

Kenya nodded her head slowly then offered the sneaky, cold grin again. "I just about fainted, but once I got over it we had a good time. A *great* time. I've never had so much sex in my life. We did it in every room on every surface. He told me he loved me and wanted me to have his baby. I never made him wear protection. It was like we were married."

"Did you get pregnant?"

"No." Kenya raised her hands and her face twitched. "That fake-butt bitch came back into the picture and he got *her* pregnant. We argued for months about that. I mean, how could he be so nasty as to sleep with her without using protection?"

Farr said, "On the other hand, how could *you* sleep with him without using protection?"

Kenya froze in the act of rearranging her hands and slowly turned her head to look at Farr. "Are you trying to be a smart ass?"

"No, not at all," Farr replied.

"Then let me tell it my way," Kenya snapped. "I came here to get this off my chest...to tell my story. I'm not here to be ridiculed or judged. If I want to be judged I'll go to a goddamn courthouse."

"Okay," Farr said.

"Okay," Kenya echoed with uneasy arrogance. She seemed to have lost the thread of her thought and her eyes wandered uneasily to the door which was firmly shut.

"Would you like that open?" Farr asked.

"No," Kenya said quickly. She gave a nervous little laugh. "What do I want to look at your secretary for?"

Farr didn't speak.

"So the fake-butt s bitch had the baby," Kenya said. She brushed at her forehead as if sketching memories. "Last November. Two or three days before Thanksgiving. But something happened before that. I heard a noise in the kitchen one night. I went out to look--the hall light was on--and...he was sitting on the floor with his back against the wall crying and drinking a glass of Hennessy. I asked if he was okay. He shook his head no. I asked if it had anything to do with the baby. Again, he shook his head no. Then, he told me what was bothering him. It was his two brothers. They had just been shot in Chicago. Ever since then he's been blaming Alexus and Blake for all his problems. He wants to destroy them. I mean, he *really* wants to destroy them. He had the fake-butt bitch tell them something yesterday...something that would let them know he's alive and well. Tomorrow morning his media tour begins. He'll be revealing to the world that he's alive. *Good Morning America, The Steve Harvey Show, TMZ Live, CNN, MSNBC, HLN.* You name it, he's booked it. He said Alexus and Blake are in big trouble if they don't pay up. Not sure what that means, but it's what he said."

"If you don't mind me asking," Farr cut in, leaning forward in her chair and resting her elbows on her desk, "what is it that has you so afraid?"

Kenya hesitated. She looked at the door again, sighed, and fidgeted. "Alexus is a savage. I know we're family and all that, but she's more than likely going to have T-Walk and every person he loves killed," she said darkly. "I'm worried she'll add me to that list."

King Rio

~Chapter 4~

"If I find out Kenya knew *anything* about this it's her ass," Alexus ranted. She was pacing the length of the living room floor with a gold-plated .50 caliber Desert Eagle in her had and a hellish fire in her eyes. "There's no way T-Walk was in hiding that long without contacting her. I bet that's why she's not answering her phone. She knows something. I'd bet money on that."

Blake was sitting in his desk chair with their one-year-old on his lap. He had on a red long- sleeve Balmain shirt, red Balmain jeans, and red Timberland boots. There were red diamonds in his earlobes, in his necklace, in his Hublot watch, and in the rings on his pinkie fingers. The diamonds in his watch were small, but the others were huge.

The two men standing on either side of Blake's chair were Brock and Enrique, the later of whom had just returned from Jacksonville, Florida. Just as Blake had guessed, T-Walk hadn't been anywhere near the Bennett Creek Apartments.

"Baby," Blake spoke up, "why are you holding that gun in here?"

"Settle down," she said. "It's not cocked. No bullet in the chamber. I'm just fucking angry right now and I want to hold my gun."

Enrique said, "We'll catch up with him within the next couple of days. I can feel it. I'm more interested in finding out how the bastard's still breathing after I blew half his head off a couple of years ago. That's what's got my mind scrambled. I've seen a lot of things in my life, but never have I seen a man come back from the dead."

"He knows way too much about the family business," Alexus said. "If he talks I'm finished. I'll be in a fed joint for the rest of my life. Not even the C.I.A. director will be able to get me out of this one."

"There's nothing to worry about," Enrique assured her.

"What the *fuck* do you mean there's nothing to worry about?"Alexus snapped, turning her head to scowl at Enrique as she continued to pace. "You must not have read the same email I read…the email he had his little girlfriend send me. You couldn't have read *that* email, not if you've come to the conclusion that there's nothing to worry over. He knows our secrets and he's willing to sell them to the highest bidder."

"Then be the highest bidder," Blake reasoned.

"Exactly," Enrique agreed. "We can really just pay him off. All he wants is a nice payday to get his feet back under him. Think of it from his perspective. He was a hot-shot TV producer, worth a few hundred million. When he was declared dead his family got everything. After all thetime that's passed I doubt if he's still set on coming after you two. He just wants to be rich again. So make him rich again. Give him a show on MTN and a hundred million. Abraham Lincoln once said that the best way to defeat an enemy is to make him your friend. Or something like that."

Alexus shook her head, gritted her teeth, and kept pacing. She wore an all-white Alexander McQueen dress that displayed every inch of her curves and snow-white Gucci boots. Her white diamonds made Blake's red diamonds look like tiny pebbles in comparison. Though she had long ago decided to wear white every day for the rest of her life, on the inside she was currently the color of fire. There was an internal struggle taking place inside of her. Something was chasing her--some dark, noxious beast of emotion with the unrelenting speed and stamina of Usain Bolt. She knew what it was.

There was a time I her past when she'd been madly in love with Trintino Walkson. In fact,he was the only other man besides Blake who'd ever had her heart. Deep down she realized she was actually kind of glad he wasn't dead. Not that she would ever consider going back to him. It was more because she felt guilty for having turned the two men against each other.

She forced herself to calm down. Handing the Desert Eagle over to Brock, she drew in a calming breath and then exhaled. *I can handle this*, she thought. "Enrique," she said, "call off the search for T-Walk. We don't need him feeling threatened. I think you're right. Partnering up with him might be the best way to go. Release the girl and send her away with a gift of…oh, let's say…ten million in cash. Apologize to her for the bump on the head she took and tell her the money goes to T-Walk."

"Our guys put a tracker on her car. Should we keep that in place?""I don't know. What do you think?"

"We should leave it. Just in case," Enrique advised. "She doesn't have what it takes to find out. More than likely it'll be stuck on that car for a year at least."

"Get her on the phone. I want a word with her before we let her go." "Yes, Ma'am," Enrique said, pulling out his smartphone.

As he dialed the number to whichever one of their men he'd put in charge of holding Ashley Hunter captive, Alexus gave him a brief head-to-toe look and then quickly moved her eyes to her husband's to keep herself out of trouble. He was a good looking Mexican man in his thirties with whom she'd had a brief affair just over a year ago when she and Blake had been going through a rough patch. When she gave Enrique control over the drug cartel he'd made the decision to follow her trend of having an all-white wardrobe and the bone-white Brooks Brothers three-piece suit he donned today looked amazing on him.

He crossed the room and stood next to her. He put the call

on speaker phone and they all listened to it ring. On the fourth ring the call was connected.

"Put the girl on the phone," Enrique said. "Boss Lady wants a word with her. And next time answer a little quicker, eh?"

"Put the boss lady on the phone," said a smooth male voice that instantly sent chills up the boss lady's vertebrae. "*I* want a word with *her*. And next time send more than three little Mexicans when you plan on holding my lady hostage, eh?"

~Chapter 5~

Only one of the three little Mexicans was dead. He lay on the cold concrete floor with his legs crossed at the ankles, his right arm at ten o'clock, his left arm at four o'clock, and his unblinking eyes looking up at the ceiling. Two inches above his left ear his skull was open. It was an exit wound about the size and shape of the circular little bowl at the end of an ice cream scooper. A chunk of brain matter sat in the middle of the bloody puddle of skull fragments next to his head like a heavy boulder in rising waters. The dead Mexican had reached for his gun and the reach had led to his death; a prime example of cause and effect. For every action there's a reaction and T-Walk had reacted swiftly.

He'd followed the black Chevy van from the limestone building on Fifth all the way to this boarded up warehouse in Lower Manhattan, being careful to stay five or six car-lengths behind in his Ford pickup. He had waited more than seven hours before bursting into the warehouse with his .45 raised and ready to fire. He'd caught the other two guys snoozing in chairs near the back door he'd entered through and after knocking one of them out cold with the butt of his gun he'd disarmed the other Mexican goon and forced the man to lead him to Ashley, which was where he murdered the reacher. Then, he'd forced the reacher's comrade to untie Ashley from the chair.

Now, he was on the dead man's phone. He and Ashley had guns trained on the two living Mexicans he'd whom he'd forced to strip naked and lie face-down on the floor. It was freezing cold in the warehouse; the two naked men were trembling on the frigid, gray floor. Ashley had put on one of their trench coats and she was still shivering with her shoulders pulled up around her ears to fight the chill.

"T-Walk?" asked the female voice that he knew belonged to Alexus.He smiled. "The one and only," he answered. "Did you miss me?" "Apparently, we did," Alexus said carefully.

T-Walk laughed. "Good one. I see what you did there. Can't say that you missed *me* though.

I was in Chicago when that boy got whacked." "Lucky you."

"Lucky me."

"So, what is it you want?"

"Not much, actually. Not from you, at least. From your company, though--that's a different story."

"Cut the shit and tell me what it is you want so we can get this over."

"How about we start with a guarantee that the mother of my only child won't be dangled over anybody's balcony in the future? Huh? Let's start with that. Then, we'll get to a guaranteeof *my* safety. *Then*, we'll get to the money. Sound fair to you?"

"Nobody's after you, T-Walk."

"Do you honestly expect me to believe that?"

"On my father's grave," Alexus said, "nobody on my team will come for you unless you come for us. The same goes for Blake and his guys. You have my word. We're here to lend you whatever kind of help you need to get yourself back into a stable environment."

"I'll need lawyers," T-Walk said, thinking. "Good lawyers.""We'll get you a whole team of lawyers."

"No, I want *your* lawyers. I want Bostic and Staples.""You got it."

"Great," T-Walk said, suddenly cheerful. "I'll be in touch." He ended the call abruptly.

Nodding his head and smiling, he pulled the trigger twice.

Both were head shots. One man's brains mixed with the other's and now there were three dead Mexicans. The gunshots reverberated throughout the warehouse. He then led the way out of the building wearing a green Notre Dame hoodie and jeans, holding the gun in his hand and looking around to make sure thereweren't any more Mexican goons lingering around.

He helped Ashley into the pickup--a Harley Davidson edition F-150--then walked around to the driver's door and got behind the wheel. He started the engine and drove off quickly, slamming through a snowbank and going the opposite way from which he'd come.

Ashley sniffled. They were moving up a side street at a steady twenty-five miles an hour. It was hard to believe he'd seen a plow pass through this street an hour ago; another two inches hadcovered it and it was drifting in. The wind picked up and began to howl, churning the snow intoa hundred weird flying shapes. The strongest gusts of wind rocked the F-150 on its springs.

When the heat really got to blowing, Ashley got the shakes harder than ever. She pulled the trench coat tight around her and her teeth clattered together as a few drops of clear mucus spilledoff the end of her nose. "What t-t-took you s-so long?" she asked.

"I wasn't sure how many of them were in there. Didn't want to bust in there and get killed. I can't keep coming back from the dead." Keeping his eyes on the road, he dipped over and pecked her on the cheek. "If they shoot *this* T-Walk in the head there won't be any coming back from that. Don't even trip, though. I got this. Only thing I'm not too sure about is my legalissues. But, I should be okay. It's not like I faked my death. And who could blame me for going underground after a man who was impersonating me was shot and killed by a sniper? No judge will lock me up. I'll be even more famous than I was before I went into hiding."

"Just…be careful." Ashley sniffed again.

"Are you forgetting who I am?" He glanced at her. "I'm T-Walk. That name carries weight.

If anything, *they* need to be careful."

~Chapter 6~

Sincere Jerrell Owens and his younger brother, Jahlil, owned numerous properties throughout Chicago's west side neighbor-hoods, but none was more lucrative for them than the tall redbrick apartment building on Douglas Boulevard. Of the ten two-bedroom apartments, nine were rented out for the reasona-ble price of $750.00 a month. The only apartment the brothers refused to rent out was the top-floor apartment where their father had lived before he passed away late last year, leaving them the building and several houses in his will. Big Man--that's what everyone had called the old man--had also left them with a little over a million dollars a piece.

In the North Lawndale neighborhood where the apartment building was located, the only young black men who were known millionaires were the Owen brothers, which explained why so many young black women in the area disregarded the fact that the brothers were both married men. There was also Bankroll Reese who was rumored to have inherited more than fifty million dollars from his Pops, but Reese was hardly ever in the neighborhood anymore. Rell and Jah, on the other hand, were in the hood every day.

It was approaching noon when the two brothers stomped the snow off of the the bottoms of their shoes and entered the apartment carrying cases of beer and bags of other party supplies. The girl who followed them in was a pretty, dark-skinned girl named Mila. Jah had picked her up at the liquor store and Rell knew his little brother wanted to fuck the girl. But, what could he say? His little bro was a grown man now.

Rell went into the kitchen, folded his leather Pelle Pelle coat over the back of a chair, and rinsed out three drinking glasses. They had two bottles of Patron to uncork and guzzle and he intended to do just that. He was putting some beers in the freezer when Mila came in and sat at the table.

"Jah went back out to the car to get those blunts," she said. "I didn't know y'all lived here.

Tamia said you and Jah had moved to a whole 'nother neighborhood."

"We did." Rell closed the freezer and looked at her. "We live in houses now with our wives.

We just keep this spot to kick it in from time to time."

"I know y'all got married, nigga." She sucked her teeth, regarding him with a sexy half-smile. "You ain't gotta rub it in my face.""Wasn't trying to rub it in your face."

"Good...because I'll fuck the shit out of you and your lil' brother and send y'all both home to your *wives*."

Rell chuckled and shook his head. He was a remarkably handsome, brown-skinned man in his mid-twenties. He had a muscular physique and a smile that had charmed the panties off of a number of pretty young women like Mila. But, all that had gone down before he'd chosen to marry Tamera Lyon and he couldn't imagine himself ever cheating on his beautiful wife.

His iPhone rang just in the nick of time. He checked it, saw that it was the big homie Juice calling, and answered the call immediately. "What up, big dog?" Rell greeted.

"Man," Juice said, "I'ma need Jah with me this weekend. Just for a day or two. We'll be back before Christmas. I really need you to come too. It's a plane trip to Cali."

"You know we always got you. What's this about?"

"You wouldn't believe me if I told you. I'm still trying to wrap my mind around it.

Bulletface wants to meet with me and my girl."

"Bulletface? The rapper?" Rell's eyebrows rose an inch.

"Yeah. I know, it fucked me up too. You know my girl used to fuck with him. He used to get money with Cup. Big money. He invited us out there to talk business and I don't wanna go by myself. I need a young, wild nigga with me. That's why I want Jah with me. Plus, I think it'll look good on our behalf, you know, if we show up looking like money…some real certifiedstreet niggas."

Rell paused to think it over. He was understandably hesitant. Not even a year and a half ago he'd come home from serving several years in Stateville prison (he'd been cellmates with Juice for five whole months of that sentence) and upon his release he had promised his mother he would never put himself in a position to be taken away from the family again. But, having an infamously trigger-happy little brother like Jah had thrown him off his path of righteousness too many times to count. While they were both members of the Traveler Vice Lords, Jah was much more involved in the gang activity. Jah was a gang-banger and he banged harder than Rell had ever banged. It had taken months of marriage and lessons from his big brother to finally calm Jah

down. Now, their only real everyday gang activity consisted of supplying their gang on 13th and Avers with drugs to sell and guns to protect themselves with. Jah had found a gun dealer in northwest Indiana. Rell bought kilos of cocaine from Juice, usually at least three or four per month and always through a third party. Lately, he'd been contemplating cutting ties with the gang to focus on starting a family with his wife. What better way to end it than with one large quantity purchase? And who better to do it with than the most famous rapper in the game?

"I'm in," he said. "Jah just ran back out to the truck, but I know he'll want to go too. All he listens to is Boosie and Bulletface. He'll be too happy to go." He poured some Patron into two ofthe glasses and pushed one to Mila, who had taken off her coat and was now digging her pinkie finger into a small bag of cocaine.

"Alright," Juice said. "The nigga texted my girl after she got off the line with him and said he'll be sending his private plane to pick us up Friday morning. That means no baggage checks, so you can bring whatever you want to bring. I'm taking my strap and a few blunts. That's all I really need."

"Did you hear her actually talking to him?" "Heard the whole thing. It was on speakerphone." "That's wild. I know that shit blew you, didn't it?""Hell yeah. Fucked my head up."

Rell squinted, thinking back to the prison cell he'd shared with Juice and then he realized something. "Wait a minute. You said Bulletface used to fuck with your girl? He used to fuckwith Bubbles? The stripper?"

"Yeah."

"Is that the same Bubbles you had taped to the wall in our cell? The model you tore out ofmy Black Lingerie magazine?"

"Yep, that's her. I told y'all I was on her ass when I got out.""Damn. Is she still thick like she was in that magazine?" Juice's reply was a laugh.

"Man," Rell said, "you got to be the luckiest nigga in the world. That girl is so thick. Mmm. Lucky nigga." He shook his head, took a gulp of tequila, and chased it down with a mouthful of beer. "I'll be at you. Just hit me up when you're ready to go."

"Yep. Solid."

"Solid." Rell ended the call and put his smartphone down on the table.

In his peripheral he saw that Mila was observing him the way a lioness might observe her prey. After a time, he could she that she was analyzing the length of him, gawking at the way his sculpted muscles stretched the fabric of his long-sleeve shirt. Her eyes moved to the front of his loose-fitting jeans and remained there until Jah strode in a moment later.

Snowflakes littered the shoulders of Jah's leather Pelle coat like dandruff. He was still as scrawny at eighteen as he'd been when he was eight. He was ten shades darker than Rell and ten times as arrogant. He picked Mila right up out of the chair and she wrapped her legs around his waist. "You wanna fuck my big brother too, don't you?"

She nodded emphatically. "He already know."

"I'm too cool. Y'all ain't 'bout to get me killed," Rell said, scooping up his phone and drinks. He gave Jah a disapproving look. "Bruh, you know how Tirzah is. If she ever finds out about this shit she'll go nuts."

"Just call and make sure they ain't left the house," Jah replied. "Let me do me, Joey Greco.

This ain't *Cheaters*, nigga." And with that Jah was off to the bedroom with Mila.

Rell heard the bedroom door shut just as he was lowering himself onto the living room sofa. He thought of how stupid his brother was to be cheating on his wife with a random hood-rat. Then, his mind went to the picture of Bubbles that had hung on the concrete wall in his and Juice's prison cell and he smiled at the memory. Then, his mind went to the trip they'd be taking to California two days from now and the smile grew even wider. He wondered if Alexus would be there. God, he hoped so. Queen A--the only black woman with more global influence than Queen Bey and just as curvy and stunningly beautiful too. Queen A, who'd ended Bill Gates' 23-year reign as America's richest person with her 2016 net worth of $82 billion; Queen A, who'd once been charged and eventually acquitted of being the boss of a Mexican drug cartel, which had essentially turned her into every dope boy's dream girl; Queen A, who had 120 million Instagram followers, one of whom was Sincere Jerrell Owens.

With a beaming smile, he took the blunt he'd rolled earlier

from the ashtray in front of him, fired it up, and dialed his wife's number. He studied the contact photo he'd assigned to her number while the phone rang, admiring her full lips, high cheekbones, and flawless chocolate- brown skin. In the phone she was neck-deep in a bubble bath he had taken the time to prepare for her last night. Like Rell, Tamera was in her early twenties and her older sister, Tirzah--Jah's wife-- was a couple of years older than her. Tirzah had the kind of body Bubbles had and she had once been a stripper at Redbone's Gentlemen's Club, which was where Bubbles worked now. Most men Rell knew considered Tirzah the sexier of the two sisters, but Rell had a different opinion. To Rell, there was nothing on earth that could compare to the sheer beauty of a dark-skinned black woman. To Rell, Tamera Owens was the sexiest woman alive. "Hey, hubby," she answered the phone.

"Y'all still at the house?" he asked a bit too quickly.

"It's a goddamn blizzard outside. I'm not going out there."

"You wanna go to L.A. for the weekend? We can stay until the new year if you want to. Bring in the new year in ninety degree weather. I can get us a nice suite, you know? Take you out somewhere nice. Just me and you. Let Jah and Tirzah come, but we'll stay in a different hotel than them Won't even let them know where we're at until it's time to leave."

Tamera laughed heartily. "You're so stupid."

"About an hour before midnight," Rell continued, "we'll return to our suite in a horse-drawn carriage...me dressed in a nice Armani suit, you in a tight-ass dress with no panties on underneath. On the elevator I'll rub on that ass, kiss on the side of your neck, the front of your neck. Nibble and kiss on those sexy lips."

"I hate you so much right now."

Rell grinned, feeling his dick hardening and growing in his True Religion jeans as he took a long drag from his blunt.

"Then, once we're back in our suite, I'll lay you down on the couch, massage your feet, tell you how much I love you and how glad I am to have you as my wife. I'll kiss on those pretty toes, kiss my way from your feet to your inner thighs, and finally to that sweet--"

A sudden knock at the door put a pause to his tantalizing New Year's Eve ideas. He got up, sat his blunt in the ashtray, drew the .40 caliber Glock from his left hip (you could never be too cautious in North Lawndale), and headed toward the door.

"Can I tell you what I'll do?" Tamara asked.

"Yeah, tell me." Rell unlocked the door and opened it. His blood shot eyes, which had been nearly shut, very quickly became like saucers. So did his mouth.

Tamera and Tirzah were standing at the door, looking at him with knowing eyes and shrugging off their heavy coats. Tirzah had one hand hidden from view.

"I'll give you a pass this time," Tamera said, slipping her smartphone into her sweatpants pocket. "That's what the fuck I'll do."

"Tell Jah and that bitch to come out here," Tirzah said and Rell saw that she had a taser in her hand, the kind you had to get up-close and personal with. "Jah!" Rell shouted. "Come and get your crazy-ass wife!" "*And bring that bitch out here with you!*" Tirzah added. "What bitch?" Rell asked, casting a leery glance at the taser.

"The bitch y'all picked up at the L," Tirzah said matter-of-factly "My bitch Smoove was there. She saw the whole thing. Jah started talking to the bitch and she left with--"

Tirzah suddenly lunged forward in an attempt to get past Rell and into the apartment. The instinct to protect his brother compelled him to try to hold her back, but the threat her taser posedkilled that thought. Tamera ran in right behind Tirzah and all Rell could do was shake his head, put the Glock back on his hip, and follow his wife and Jah's wife into the apartment. He kicked the door shut and took giant leaps, bounding first through the living room and then into the kitchen just as a door slammed shut. He heard the first sharp crackling of electricity as he entered the short hall that led to two bedrooms, a bathroom, and a linen closet at the far end.

Poor Mila. She was on the floor, taking brutal kicks to the face from Tamera and Tirzah.

Blood began to soar into the air. Jah seemed to have looked himself in the bedroom. "Come get your bitch, Jah," Tirzah kept saying.

Rell closed his fingers tightly around Tamera's elbow and yanked her into the kitchen while at the same time shoving Tirzah so hard she went flying into the wooden door of the linen closet.

"Lil' bruh!" Rell shouted.

Finally Jah eased open the bedroom door. "Tirz, don't touch me with that taser," he said. "Oh, you're good." Tirzah came toward Rell and offered him the weapon. "Here you go.

Take it." But as Rell was reaching for it she lowered it to her side. Tears welled in her eyes, glistening like the melted snowflakes in her hair. She turned to Jah. "I hope you know this marriage is over."

"Baby, let me explain what the fuck just happened," Jah said, slowly moving out of the bedroom. His alert eyes shifted from Tirzah to Mila (who was beginning to stir a little) and back to Tirzah.

There was another electric crackling sound. Tirzah thrust the taser at Jah, who immediately jumped back. "*Get* the fuck away from me," she snapped. She breezed past Rell and then she and Tamera left the apartment with blood splattered on the toes of their boots.

"Stupid ass," Rell said as Jah appeared in front of him. "I warned you about this shit. I *told* you." He stepped back into the hall and both of them looked at Mila. She was up on her hands and knees, her mouth a running faucet of blood.

"Wifey damn near got shot," Jah said.

"No nigga," Rell corrected. "*You* damn near got *zapped.*"

King Rio

~Chapter 7~

Alexus had just finished bathing and dressing little Juan when Blake came walking into the bedroom with their five-year-old son King Neal clinging to his leg. She looked over her shoulder at them.

"Ma!" King said. "Daddy won't let me...um...he won't give me a piggyback ride. Can you help me beat him up?"

"How about I beat up you *and* your daddy?"

"Hold on now," Blake said, grinning. "Y'all ain't 'bout to be bating up on me."

Alexus put Juan down on the carpet, sat down on the bed, and watched the toddler stumble his way toward his father and brother. King Neal unglued himself from Blake's leg and scooped his little brother up. Blake sat down next to Alexus and then leaned back, propping himself up onan elbow.

"T-Walk hasn't been back on our radar for a good forty-eight hours," Alexus said, "and he's already killed three of our men."

"Your men," Blake said.

"Well, my men. Same difference. I'm starting to second guess my decision to help him."

"In his defense, we did kidnap his girlfriend. All he did was find her and did what he had todo to get her back."

Alexus gave him a look. "So you're defending him? After all the times you and him havetried to kill each other, you're actually defending him?"

"Not defending him. Just saying what's real. If a nigga snatched you up and held you insome warehouse I'd do the same thing."

"Whatever. You missed having him around.""You got me fucked up"

She snickered and picked up her iPhone. Not many people had her cell phone number, but she had a bunch of texts from the ones who did. Nikkia Staples, a partner at one of the most prestigious law firms in the country had sent her a text message expressing shock and disbelief at the whole T-Walk situation. There were two text messages from her mother, Rita Mae Bishop, who was on a flight from Madrid that would be landing at JFK any minute now. Rita wanted to know if the kids were dressed and ready to go. They were going to spend Christmas together at Rita's new Calabasas mansion. The children's gifts were stacked up around the huge tree in her foyer and (according to the texts) she didn't have time for any of Alexus and Blake's foolishness.

"King," Alexus said, "go in there and see if your sister is ready to go. Granny's at the airportwaiting on us."

"Yay! Grandma!" King threw his fists in the air, grinning his father's grin. He had been on his knees in front of Juan and was just getting to his feet when Savaria appeared in the doorway.

The nine-year-old didn't say a word. She simply leaned a shoulder against the door frame with her head lowered, eyes on her iPhone 6 Plus (she would get the 7 Plus on Christmas morning), and her scalp an intricate map of cornrows. She was dressed in a black Dolce & Gabbana jumpsuit and there was something about her that set off an alarm in her step-mom's brain. Alexus couldn't put her finger on it, not just yet, but she was certain--absolutely, unwaveringly certain--that something was wrong.

"Hey, Vari," Alexus said, trying to sound welcoming. "You excited to get back to California? Got all your stuff packed?"

Savaria didn't move a single muscle. Not one. "Is some-thing wrong?" Alexus asked.

Nothing; Savaria stood there as if Sub Zero from *Mortal*

Kombat had blasted her with a ball of body-freezing liquid ice.

Blake sat up. "Oh, so you can't hear nobody today, huh? You done all of a sudden went deaf? That's okay. That's okay because when Santa Claus calls me back and asks about that Christmas list of yours, guess who's gonna be deaf then." He leaned forward. "If you don't raise your head and look me in my face I'm going to take that phone and break it in half." He said it very politely with the clear and precise pronunciation of an English teacher.

Slowly, Savaria's head rose. She sighed heavily as her eyes met his and Alexus finally knewwhat it was about Vari that had set the alarm off in her head a moment earlier. It was *black.* Savaria hadn't worn the color in almost a year. She liked dressing in all-white like Alexus. Asidefrom the maroon shirt and tan slacks she had to wear to school, she'd been wearing nothing but white everyday. So what had changed? What had Alexus done to make the little girl stop lookingup to her.

"Did I do something to you?" Alexus asked.

Savaria kept her lips sealed and her eyes on Blake who chuckled and pulled at the small patch of hair under his bottom lip. "I take it you're mad at Alexus for some reason," he said."Am I right?"

Savaria nodded.

"Can you tell her *why* you're mad at her?" She shook her head no.

"Can you tell *me* why?"

Savaria's expression became thoughtful. Then, with another sigh, she said, "Daddy, she's cheating on you."

"I'm *what*?" This was news to Alexus.

Frowning, Blake turned to Alexus. "You cheating on me?"

"Yes, she is," Vari said. "She's cheating on you with some guy named Mandinko Warner. He sounded like he's from Africa or something. She told him he had to leave before you gotback home."

Blake and Alexus were already laughing. King Neal started laughing for no real reason otherthan the fact that his parents were laughing and Juan copied his big brother's laugh.

Savaria stood in the doorway looking puzzled. "Am I missing something here?" she asked. When no one replied, she added, "You people are seriously weird. Mentally unfit to be parents, in my opinion. And your weirdness is rubbing off on my little brothers."

"I'm not…cheating…on your father," Alexus said between laughs.

"Then who is Mandinko?" Finally, Vari chuckled and smiled. "I'm dumb, aren't I? I said something stupid." She shook her head.

"That was your father I was talking to."

"That's what I get for being nosy. Sorry, Ma." Her smile broadened.

"I forgive you. Take your brothers and turn on the video game. Make sure you give Kingand Juan a controller." Alexus glanced over at Blake, who was lying flat on his back now, laughing breathlessly with tears rolling down the sides of his face. "Let me and a Mandinko over here get a few minutes of privacy."

As soon as the kids were gone Alexus went to the door and locked it. "We need to get this door sound-proofed," she said as she returned to the bed and climbed onto Blake's lap.

Looking down at his handsome dark-brown face as he fought to contain his laughter, Alexusplanted her hands on his chest and sucked her bottom lip in between her teeth. Tall, tatted up, and impossibly muscled, Blake's incredible body never failed to get her vaginal juices flowing. He was a good-looking (hell, *fine*-looking) young black man who was wanted by most young women and he was all hers. No more staying up late at night wondering whose bed he was in. No more sharing him with groupies. No more sending armed hit-men after side-chicks who respected sacred marriage vows about as much as a Ku Klux Klan member respected the Black Lives Matter movement.

"That was funny," he said, wiping his eyes. He recognized the hungry look on his face's face and shook his head. "No. Nuh-uh. Mandinko Warner has left the building."

"Mandinko's gonna get himself fucked up if he so much as grins at that girl when he meets with her in California. Then he'll *really* leave the building."

"She has a boyfriend."

"And? You had a wife when you fucked her." "That was different."

"Nigga, I will--" she put her hands on his throat, "strangle the life out of you. Is that what you want me to do?"

He nodded, but she let go of his neck; no sense in damaging the goods. She lowered her mouth to his and kissed him instead of strangling him. He kissed her back. His strong black fingers pressed into the flesh of her ass and he stood up, forcing her to her feet with him. He turned her around, yanked up her dress, and lifted her knees up onto the bed with an animal-like quickness. He smacked her on the ass a couple of times, a habit of his that she'd grown used to over the years. He loved her big, round ass just as much as she loved his long, fat dick.

"Don't start yelling and shit," he said.

"I won't. I'll be quiet." She'd sew her mouth shut if that what it took to get what she wanted right now-- what she *needed* right now.

Blake wasted no time in giving her what she needed. He pushed in the bulbous head and kept pushing, rocking back and forth, getting deeper and deeper with every thrust of his hips. He established a steady, pounding rhythm and didn't let up. A minute later, Alexus broke her vow of silence when a brief moan burst from her mouth. A second moan came right after the first one, but she managed to barricade it behind tightly sealed lips. He bent over the arch of her back and kissed it; a big kiss, not a little one. A smacky kiss. Then, he balled the fingers of one hand into her hair, pulled her head back, and fucked her like a madman on Viagra.

~Chapter 8~

Thursday, December 22nd

"Five more months and you'll officially be a granddad," Bubbles said with a sarcastic smile."Aren't you excited?"

"Absolutely," Juice replied drably from the driver's seat. "Just jumping for joy over here.

Can't you hear it in my voice?"

Bubbles laughed. They were in his Jaguar F-Pace barreling down 16th Street in the exotic looking silver SUV past snow-banks as tall as Ra'Mya and pedestrians bundled in multiple layers of clothing. The snowstorm had passed but the wind-chill factor was a son-of-a-bitch. The wind moaned, howled, and whistled through the streets, throwing snow against the exterior of the F- Pace. It was just 7:30 P.M. and already the sun had departed. Most of the buildings on either side of the street had grown black and menacing. The SUV's head-lights cut through the hissinggloom like gas lamps on a coal-dark night.

"I can't wait," Bubbles said, "to step off that plane and into the everyday sunshine of California. I'm a Midwest girl to the heart, but ain't nothing like that west coast weather."

"As long as it's not as hot as it was in Vegas back in September. That was the most miserable two weeks of my life."

"No. Don't even jinx us like that. Vegas was only misera-ble because we weren't sure whether or not you'd be wanted for murder when we made it back into Illinois. This trip is going to be fucking magical." She thumbed through her iPhone. "He got us a presidential suite at the Four Seasons in

Hollywood that costs, listen to this, $9,800.00 a night. We'll be up in that bitch living like him and Alexus! I can't believe it. The plane will be ready for take off at 5:30 in the morning. That's ten hours away."

"What about rooms for Rell and Jah?"

"He's giving us a credit card to use while we're there. Not that Rell and Jah would need Blake's help in getting a room anyway."

"You text them the info?"

"Of *course* I did. Sent it to Tamera. She said her, Rell, and Jah will be there at the airport at 5:30 sharp and her sister, Tirzah, *might* be there, but she's not sure yet. I guess Tirzah caught Jah with another woman yesterday and she hasn't spoken to him since. She made him get out and everything. He slept at Tamera and Rell's house last night while his side chick spent the night in the hospital. They say her eye got knocked out of the socket, she lost a few teeth, and got hernose and jaw broken. Suffice it to say, she got the beat down of the century."

Glancing over at Bubbles as he made a left turn onto Trumbull Avenue, Juice had to grin. The 27-year-old woman shared many of his daughter, Dawn's, qualities--originality, confidence, wit, charm, and above all, that electric lack of disappointment that suggested that nothing in them had yet dimmed and perhaps nothing ever would. In the presence of such a force field, thebackup generators of his own energy switched on suddenly, sending surges of possibilities through his psyche. He suspected it was this sensation, even more than youth or beauty, that had always drawn men to younger women.

His eyes went back to the street. He pulled over at the end of the block at the 15th Street intersection. It was a one-way street where him and his late friend, Cup, alias Red-D, had started gang-banging and selling drugs way back in the early 1990s. There was a red Chevy Suburban parked on the other side of the street; its driver and passenger doors swung open the moment Juice parked. The young black man with dreadlocks who got out of the driver's seat had on a heavy red Pelle Pelle jacket and his name was Wayno. He was a high-ranking TVL who managed the mob's daily activities and brought the cash from drug sales (lately it had been around $20,000.00 a day) directly to Juice. The boy who got out of the passenger's seat was the mean-spirited 16-year-old Jamal Cushenberry and his thin gray Nike jacket was stained and torn in some places. He was the kid Wayno had asked Juice to come over and have a talk with.

Bubbles said, "I thought we were going to dinner. What are we doing here?"

"We'll be gone in a second," Juice said, lowering his window as Wayno and Jamal approached.

Usually Wayno extended his hand for a gang-related shake whenever he walked up to Juice, but the biting cold dissuaded him from doing so this time; his hands stayed buried in his coat pockets. "You need to talk to this lil' nigga here," Wayno said.

"About what?" Juice looked at Jamal. "Fuck I need to talk to you about?"

"I'll let y'all talk," Wayno said. "It's too damn cold to be standing out here." He ran back to the Suburban.

Jamal said, "Man, that nigga Jah and his girl jumped my sister Mila yesterday. I asked Wayno for a pistol so I could go and deal with that nigga and I'm *still* on that. Period. Wayno said I can't do it 'cause Jah a Traveler. I ain't tryna hear none of that shit, on God."

"You sure it was Jah who did that to your sister?"

"Am I *sure*?" He looked up at Juice blankly and wiped the end of his nose. "I know for a *fact* it was Jah and his girl.

Jah set my sister up, talked her into coming to that building on Douglas and Homan with him and his brother. Then his girl came in and they jumped my sister."

"I don't think it happened like that." "That's how it went down."

"I don't think so," Juice persisted.

"I'm telling you what it is. Mila ran the whole shit down to me. She can barely even talkwith her mouth all wired shut like it is, but she told me what happened from start to finish." He wiped his nose again, scowling. A dark-skinned, nappy-headed teenager with a grudge, he hadhis mind set. He wanted Jah's life.

"Do me a favor," Juice said. "Go home, sit down, and give yourself some time to think this over because you're making a huge mistake and Jah is not one to be--"

"Maaaan, *fuck* Jah!" Jamal snapped. Then, he looked to his right in the direction from whichJuice had come. A millisecond later he turned to his left and ran. At least that's what he tried to do. He made it around the front of the F-Pace and onto the curb before slushy snow took his feet from under him and sent him baseball-sliding onto the sidewalk.

Jah was on him in a flash. *Flash* was definitely the word. At one moment Jah was streaking past Juice's window and then at the next he was standing over Jamal with a gun in his hand, shooting the boy in the head. One, two, three, four, five quick shots, stentorian in the previously silent night.

Juice shifted into drive and drove off in a hurry.

~ ~ ~

Forty-five minutes later they made it into downtown and Juice pulled into the parking lot in front of Great Aunt Micki's, the only eatery on Michigan Avenue open at this late hour. Hechose a booth in back where he had a good view of the door and plate-glass window. Instinct had taken over without him even being fully aware of it. Bubbles draped her full-length fur coat over the back of her seat and sat staring out of the window streaked with light and the ghostly reflection of faces. He waited, then ordered for both of them: Pepsi soda, steak, shrimp, home fries (for him), and wheat toast.

When the food arrived, her eyes came back into focus. "I don't like shrimp," she said. Juice reached over and moved her shrimp onto his plate. "You like steak, don't you?" She stared at him.

"Do you want something else with it?" "I like fries."

Without a word, he used a spoon to transfer most of his home fries to her plate. He smiled at her as he began to eat, periodically admiring the way her black Fendi jumpsuit hugged her every curve.

An old couple paid their bill and left. A middle-aged man with a giant wobbly gut entered, made his way to the counter with his buttocks overflowing the stool, and ordered catfish and spaghetti. A young, heavily made-up woman with a lot of hair stood outside smoking. One hip was canted out of her long coat; her leather skirt barely covered her upper thighs. *That bitch gotta be freezing*, Juice thought. A car pulled up and Juice tensed. The heavily made-up woman stubbed out her cigarette and walked on stiletto heels toward the car. The passenger door opened and with a practically liquid move she slid in. The car drove off and Juice exhaled softly and went back to his food. Inside of the soul food restaurant there were perhaps a dozen other characters. No one seemed to pay anyone else the slightest attention.

"Baby, talk to me," Juice said after a time.

She continued to eat with an eerie kind of mechanical precision as if she knew she was required to fuel the system but was tasting nothing. Her gaze was neither on him nor on her food, but was focused on something--or someone--he would never be able to see.

He had just gobbled down his last four home fries when she suddenly spoke. "It's just that, you know, he looked so young."

"I tried to warn him. I told him not to fuck with Jah."

"So, that makes it okay?" As if she had just noticed the food, she dropped her fork with a clatter and pushed the plate away in a gesture of disgust. "This tastes like soggy dog balls."

Juice laughed. "How you know what soggy dog balls taste like?"She stared him mutely.

"I'm sorry you had to see that lil' dude lose his life like that. Okay? I really am sorry you had to see that. But, you gotta remember w here you're at. This Chicago life ain't nothing to be played with. You can't just go around saying you're going to kill somebody and expect them not to react. I would've done the same thing."

"You're an idiot, you know that?" she replied vehemently. "You think you have it all figured out, but you don't. It's not normal to resort to murder under any circumstances that's not self-defense. I don't give a damn what city we're in. Jah's a fucking lunatic, you're a fucking lunatic! Every person who's contributed to the more than six hundred murders in this fucked up city this year is a fucking lunatic."

"Same thing I said when they killed my son. And when I called home from the joint and found out Cup and Lil Cholly got killed."

A tense silence rose between them, bristling with the defensive thorns they brought out in each other. Her disposition seemed to have softened a little with Juice's mention of his murdered son, but she remained defiant, holding his unwavering gaze until finally the light in his head clicked on.

"Wait," he said. "You think I had something to do with Jamal getting killed, don't you?"

"I find it mighty funny how you pulled up and tried to talk him out of killing Jah right before Jah came out of nowhere and shot him. And look at what Wayno did. He brought that boy to your window and then got his ass right back in that Suburban. How am I *not* supposed to find that whole situation a little suspicious?"

Juice reached in a front pocket of his black Balmain jeans and took out his iPhone. He went through the text message Wayno had sent him and showed it to Bubbles. "You see that? It says, 'Big homie, come and talk to this lil' nigga Jamal. He trippin and won't listen to me.' See the time on that? 7:21. That means I pulled up not even ten minutes later. No way I could've been involved in that shit. If I would've had a say in it, believe me, I would not have let it go down like that. Not on my block. But like I said before, I don't blame my lil' homie Jah. He found out a nigga was talking about killing him, so he made the first move. To be honest, Jamal was dumb for making the threat. Everybody knows that Jah is not to be fucked with. I've been on this earth for thirty-five years and I honestly can't name one person who's more dangerous to his enemies than Jah. I really can't. That's why I wanted to bring him with us to Cali. I know that if anything pops off while we're there Jah will go all out."

Another silence ensued, but the frigid mask of beauty Bubbles had worn moments prior had now thawed. A tiny, barely there smirk played around the corners of her mouth.

Juice held out a hand, palm up. "Why don't we make a pact to never jump to conclusions about anything in this relationship, no matter what?"

For a long moment, she did nothing. The way her eyes searched his face made him think that she was trying to get a sense of whether his offer was genuine.

She drew herself up and her expression became more relaxed. "How much money do you have altogether right now? And how much more do you need before you finally give that street life up?"

"Hopefully this Cali trip will be the end for me. I got about two million now. Another eight and I'll call it a day. I'll fall back and let Wayno run shit."

"I hope so. If I have to give up stripping, you have to give up dealing." She extended her hand until it rested lightly in his. She looked at him, her eyes glittery, magnified by burgeoning tears. "I don't want to lose you. Ever. Not to the prison system, not to an early grave, not to anything. Do you understand that?"

He nodded. "I do," he said and immediately envisioned himself repeating those same words to her sometime in the near future.

~ ~ ~

Back in the Jaguar, he brought up the topic that had been spreading like a California wildfire since early that morning: the news that one of the most successful black television producers in history, thought to have been assassinated years ago, was in fact very much alive. It was without a doubt the most shocking news to hit the media since last month's election of Donald Trump.

"So, T-Walk's been alive this whole time," he said. " I wonder what Alexus thinks about that."

"That's what everybody's talking about on social media," Bubbles said, that familiar cheer returning to her voice as she thumbed through her iPhone. "It's the number one trending topic on Twitter *and* Facebook and 'T-Walk's back' is the most popular hashtag on Instagram. All the celebrities are posting about it. E-40 said now all we need is for Tupac to come out of hiding." She laughed her sweet laugh and slapped her knee.

"Blake absolutely hated T-Walk. A lot of people think their beef actually started over Alexus and that it might have been T-Walk who sent those guys to shoot Blake in 2011. It's crazy because the first time me and Blake hooked up was the same night he got shot up. It was Christmas Eve."

"I don't wanna hear that shit."

"Awww. Is that jealousy I hear in your voice?" She leaned towards him, lips poised for a kiss. "Give me some sugar, you jealous old granddaddy."

"Nah, I'm cool on that one," Juice said, leaning away from her. "I'm not interested in kissing anybody who knows what soggy dog balls taste like."

King Rio

~Chapter 9~

Tirzah knew her husband like she knew herself and when she saw on Facebook that the boy who'd posted that he was going to shoot her and Jah had been shot and killed on 15th and Trumbull a few hours ago, she instantly knew who had committed the murder. Knowing that Jah

had gone to such lengths to protect them warmed her heart. She forgave him for the Mila

Cushenberry incident, but he wasn't in the clear just yet. He was going to pay for what he'd done. One way or the other, he was going to pay for breaking her heart.

It was an hour before midnight and Tirzah was pacing a tight circle in the kitchen of her and Jah's four-bedroom home, which was just around the corner from Rell and Tamera's house. She had on a Moncler sweater over jeans and Air Max sneakers. She was nursing a glass of Grey Goose vodka through a bendy straw, feeling a rising anger at Jah for yesterday's infidelity yet knowing that she was only pissed at him because he wasn't there with her now (even though it had been her who'd made him get out).

Holding her smartphone in one manicured hand, she went to her sister's number. She hesitated and then dialed.

Tamera answered on the first ring as if she had been waiting for Tirzah's call. "Tirz, are you coming to L.A. with us or not?"

"I don't know," Tirzah said. "Where's he at?"

"Jah smoked a blunt with us and went to sleep about an hour ago. He tried calling you twice."

"I blocked his number."

"Yeah, he told us. You need to talk to that boy. Blocking his number is not the way you should be going to fix this. He's young, Tirz. He's eighteen and you're damn near thirty."

"That's no excuse. He fucked that bitch."

"So, you're gonna give her the power to ruin your relation-ship? Because that's what you're doing, whether you know it or not. I don't wanna hear you complaining if he gets caught up withsome California chick because you pushed him away."

Tirzah's pacing came to an end and she faced the sink, gazing out of the window at her snow-covered backyard. She wanted to cry. She wanted to be held and told that everything was going to be okay.

"You need to bring your ass over here and get your man. We'll be on a plane to L.A. at 5:30 tomorrow morning. I'd advise you to be on that plane with us." There was an uncom-fortable silence. "Tirzah, are you okay?"

"I'm fine. I'm already packed and ready to go."

"Want me to come over and help get your stuff in the car?"
"It's in the trunk already."

"Are you drunk?"

"I'm drinking. Wouldn't necessarily call it drunk, though. I'm trying to figure out a plan to teach him a lesson. I have some ideas. Some *good* ones too. Bet he won't try that shit again."

"Oh Jesus."

"Wanna hear them?"

"No," Tamera said. "What I want you to do is get over here so we can all be ready to leave first thing in the morning."

"I know you're lying about us going there to meet Bullet-face."

"No, you *think* I'm lying. Text Bubbles and ask her if you don't believe me. He's flying usin on his private jet. You know Bubbles used to fuck with him."

Tirzah headed out of the kitchen, through the dining room, and into the living room. "That lucky bitch," she said. "Bulletface is so damn fine. I'd ride that dick even if he wasn't a billionaire." She sat down heavily on the sofa.

"You'd be no better than Jah if you did that."

"Oh please. You mean to tell me you wouldn't fuck--"

"That's not what I said. See, me and Rell have an understanding when it comes to shit like this. We made the rules on our honeymoon. We each have four celebrities we can fuck without itbeing considered cheating. His were Rihanna, Lauren London, Alexus, and KeKe Palmer. Mine were LeBron, Usher, Drake, and Bulletface. You should've made that kind of deal with Jah."

"Jah would beat my ass if I even thought about saying something like that." Tirzah laughed. "I'll be over there in ten minutes. Leave the front door open for me."

"Okay. Hurry up." Tamera hung up.

Tirzah got up, went to the living room window, and looked out. Her mind seemed numb as the traffic passing her house was a distant buzz. A small car pulled into the driveway across the street and a couple of drunken teenagers tumbled out and loped through the snow into their parents' house. A large truck rumbled away from the gas station at the corner and back onto the slick road. Her eyes registered these small comings and goings without comment from her mind, as if she were in a theater watching a film.

After some thought, she finished off her drink, stuffed the three things she needed to getback at her husband into her purse, turned off the kitchen and bathroom lights, and headed out of the door. It was cold but she didn't regret not wearing a coat; the icy breeze was sobering and shewanted to be as sober as possible when she confronted Jah. She walked with her neck turtled down between her shoulders. A couple of boys in a top-down Mustang--it was nowhere near top- down weather--passed her as she was turning onto Grace Street. One whistled and Tirzah gave him the finger. He laughed and applauded as the Mustang accelerated down Grace.

She found Tamera waiting with the door held open. She ran up the porch stairs, slipped on a patch of ice, and would have gone down if Tamera hadn't rushed out the door and grabbed her elbow.

"You drunk bitch," Tamera said and they both laughed. She led Tirzah inside and closed the door. "Jah's upstairs, first door on the right. Me and Rell are going to bed. I'd advise you to get some rest because we'll be up at five."

"Okay." Tirzah climbed the stairs on her toes, holding on to the railing to keep her balance. Her smile grew wider and wider with every step she took and when she reached the second floor she let out a laugh that was silent aside from the breath that came out with it.

The door to the bedroom Jah was sleeping in was half way open. Tirzah tried to slither in without opening it any further, but her butt was too big. The hinges must have been well-oiled because they made nary a sound as the door opened wider.

Jah was asleep on the bed fully dressed and facing the wall that one side of the bed rested against. The lower half of a 30-round clip protruded from beneath the pillow that he wasn'tlaying on. Tirzah tip-toed to the head of the bed, tugged the clip and the Glock handgun it was attached to from under the pillow, and then dropped it in her purse. Then, she turned to the dresser, removed the three items from her purse, and laid them side by side on the dresser-top. She dug her cigarette lighter out of the rear left pocket of her jeans and unwrapped the first item-

-a pack of Black Cat Firecrackers.

She thumbed the wheel of her cigarette lighter, lit the fuse, and tossed the firecrackers onto the pillow Jah's head was on. Smiling, she spun around, picked up her other two items--a can of pepper spray and her taser-- and turned back to look at Jah just as the firecrackers started exploding behind his head.

Startled awake by the loud pops, he rolled over, came face to face with the exploding firecrackers, and then sat up, throwing himself back against the wall with his eyes wide. He was just turning to look at Tirzah when she put the taser to his ankle and sent thousands of volts surging through him. At the same time, she sprayed his face, burning his eyes with the pepper solution.

"You wanna cheat on *me*? You wanna play with my motherfuckin' *health*!" She was enraged and screaming. "Let me burn you first! Show you how the shit feels before you have mypussy all burnt up!"

She turned and ran out of the bedroom, nearly colliding with Rell and Tamera as they came running up the stairs. She moved past them and kept going. Tamera made a u-turn in the middle of the staircase and followed her.

"What the fuck was all that?" Tamera asked in a high-pitched tone. "Were those fireworks?"

They stopped at the foot of the stairs and looked up to the second floor. There was a lot of coughing going on up there. Tirzah coughed twice and sneezed one.

"What the fuck did you just do?" Tamera asked.

"Got me some payback," Tirzah said. "Bet his ass won't cheat again."

King Rio

~Chapter 10~

Friday, December 23rd

When Juice and Bubbles arrived at O'Hare International Airport it was 5:45 A.M. and the temperature was a bone-chilling twenty-two degrees. A flight attendant who looked like the Kisha character from the movie *Belly* led them out to a long white business jet.

"Your four friends boarded about ten minutes ago," the Kisha look-alike said as they approached the red-carpeted stairs with Juice rolling two suitcases along behind him.

The word *Gulfstream* was stenciled in maroon lettering underneath the window at the nose of the plane and *G650* was stenciled on the tail-wing. Juice wondered how much it cost to fuel this behemoth private jet. Probably somewhere between fifteen and twenty-five grand, he surmised.

There were two flight attendants. The Kisha look-alike's name was Gloria and the Hispanic woman's name was Olivia. The chief pilot was a bald and cadaverous man named Herbert who quickly revealed that Gloria was his daughter. "A beautiful gift from an ugly marriage," he said as Juice and Bubbles sat down in spacious, sumptuous white leather seats that faced each other with a table between them.

Tamera and Tirzah waved at them and offered good mornings. Rell, seated next to Tamera, gave a nod. Jah sat alone in the far back of the jet; his eyes looked red and irritated, his face mildly swollen, and his nose puffy. Juice didn't ask.

Herbert said, "You, my friends, are about to take a ride in the G650, the finest business aircraft ever conceived, designed, and put into production. The only purpose-built large-cabin business jet able to fly seven thousand nautical miles at a Mach

0.85 cruise speed, connecting New York to Dubai or Beijing to Dallas nonstop. The G650 can also fly six thousand nautical miles at nine-tenths the speed of sound, connecting to Los Angeles to London in record time. This aircraft has one of the most comfortable cabins available with the largest cabin windows, the largest cabin cross-section, the lowest cabin noise level, and the highest cabin pressurization of *any* purpose-built business jet. Even flying at the maximum altitude of fifty-one thousand feet, you'll feel as though you're cruising at no more than five thousand feet. All the while, fresh air will continuously circulate throughout the cabin, leaving you all feeling refreshed upon arrival to your destination."

"Nigga, fly the plane," Tirzah said impatiently.

Her outburst made everyone, even the flight attendants, laugh out loud. Herbert got a laugh out of it too.

"Okay, okay," Herbert said, showing an old man's grin as he turned and stalked off into the cockpit, but not before adding that everyone should enjoy the exquisite comforts of the jet's sixteen panoramic windows, one hundred percent fresh air replenishment system, and lie-flat seating.

As soon as Herbert was out of earshot, Bubbles spun around in her seat and gave Tirzah a look. "Girl, please let that man talk when he wants to talk. Please remember that he is our pilot."

"For real," Tamera added. "I am not trying to get nine-elevened today. He can talk for as long as he wants to talk."

"Well, I got a Grey Goose hangover," Tirzah said, reclining her seat, "and the last thing I wanna hear is every detail about this goddamn plane. If I need to know some shit like that I'll ask Siri."

"She's crazy," Bubbles muttered to Juice. "It's all good," Juice said.

"No, I mean crazy-crazy. Britney Spears with the umbrella

crazy. Mental hospital, straight- jacket crazy. I used to work with her at Redbone's. She beat up about half of the girls that dancedthere at the time."

"I heard about her." Juice eyed the generous swells of his woman's butt as she stood up and took off her coat.

Bubbles was wearing a white Ralph Lauren sweater and hip-hugging jeans. Her hair, which seemed to change colors a dozen times a month, was black with blonde highlights and was styled in a short neck-long bob. She was wearing My Burberry perfume and he was wearing Mr. Burberry cologne, the newest fragrances from Burberry.

"Baby, you look so fucking good. It's like you get prettier and prettier every day. And that ass…good God, God is *good*."

"Pervert." She smirked, sat back down, and crossed her legs real lady-like. "I sincerely hope I made the right decision by trusting your daughter to watch Ra'Mya. You know I'm protectiveof my baby."

"She's good with Dawn. Dawn's the good twin. It's the pregnant one you have to worryabout."

"I hope so."

One of the flight attendants came by with water, tea, juice, and coffee, but they declined. "Is there any Hennessy and is it okay to smoke weed?" Juice asked.

"Yes and yes," Gloria said with an indelible smile.

Soon after, Juice and Bubbles were both high and tipsy. The others must have had a long night for they were fast asleep mere minutes after the Gulfstream took to the air.

After a while, Bubbles said, "We need to come up with some kind of business to help you launder all that money. I know you got the hair salon for Shawnna and Dawn, but you need another cash business. Like a laundromat or something. It's not good to have so much cash on hand that you can't explain if the feds were ever to get a-hold of it."

"A laundromat." Juice nodded, gazing at the string of smoke rising up from the burning end of his blunt. "Might not be a bad idea."

"It's actually a great idea. I know a dope boy from Milwaukee who has five laundromats in Wisconsin. He comes to the club all the time. I think you should tell Blake to buy you a nightclub too, as part of the deal, you know? So you can have another legitimate source of income. That way you'll be able to make big money with him without bringing too much heat on the real situation. If not a nightclub then maybe a car dealership. Something worth one or two million. Tell him it takes money to make money. I doubt if he'll turn you down. If he's looking for some kind of pipeline to flood the streets of Chicago with dope, there's somebody behind him…somebody a lot more powerful than he is. I'd bet money it's his wife. Either her or that drug cartel her dad went to prison for running."

"Shit, I need a cartel plug. Two or three good moves with them and I can fall back for good. Just me, you, and the kiddos." He smiled at her and leaned forward over the thin, glossy wooden table. He liked her scent; it made him pleasantly woozy and he was only too happy to surrender himself to this voluptuous feeling. "I always knew that…one day…I'd find a woman like you. A good woman who was actually worth my time. The kind of woman who would keep me on my toes. I see that in you. You're my rider."

"I just want us to win. I want us to get to the point one day when we can own a G650. That's why I'm so determined to get you to set a goal to get out of the streets before it's too late. I've seen so many real niggas fall victim to the streets. One minute they had all the power in the world and the next they were slumped over in their cars or laid out on the sidewalk. One minute they had a million dollars, the next day they had a hundred years. Shit is real out there. Especially with all the gang-banging going on all across the city. You need an exit strategy. You've had a good run. Make these last moves with Blake and then get out before you strike out."

Juice fell back in his seat and rubbed his belly. He had on a gray Louis Vuitton skullcap, gray sweater, black jeans, and gray and white Jordan sneakers. A laugh escaped him as he observed Bubbles looking at his round belly and running her tongue along her top lip. "And I'm the pervert?" he asked.

"I like fat bellies on men," she said, sipping from her glass of iced cognac. "I don't know why, I just do. Might be because I had a crush on Biggie back in the day."

"Guess I won't be hitting the gym any time soon."

"You don't need to hit the gym. You're in perfect shape, in my opinion. Bald and round.

You got me forever, Big Daddy."

"I see you got jokes today." He leaned forward and extinguished the blunt roach. Then, he poured himself another drink--just half a glassful this time.

Bubbles was silent for some time but her eyes were busy as if she was trying to work out a particularly difficult problem. She took a deep breath, let it out slowly and deliberately, and then finally looked at him and spoke very softly. "I'm falling in love with you."

"And I'm doing the same thing," Juice said immediately. "What are we doing?"

"We're doing what grownups do. We're doing what we're supposed to be doing. You don'tfeel that way?"

"I feel like I'm giving you all of me without asking for anything in return. That's how I feel.

Do you think that's selfish of me?"

He shook his head. "I don't think it's selfish at all. I think what you need to do is figure out exactly what it is you want out of me and present it to me. I'm easy to work with. Pretty sure we'll come to some kind of compromise. Shit, I might need something from you too."

"Oh yeah?" She smirked."Mmmhmm."

"Something like what?" "Can't tell you right here."

"Then where can you tell me? Because I'm *very* interested in knowing what it is you want out of me."

Juice stood up, grinning deviously. He took her hand in his, led her down the aisle past their napping associates, and into the business jet's restroom. Her face was one big smile as he shut and locked the door. He lifted her up by the waist and sat her down on the white marble sink. Immediately, he began to kiss her on the mouth, on the chin, on the jaw, and on the neck. He inhaled through his nose the erection-inspiring scent of her perfume and within seconds the front of his pants was poking out.

He took a step back. "Take that belt off. Take them jeans off. Panties too." His tone of voicewas stern and authoritative; hungry.

She unbuckled her Hermes belt, thumbed her jeans and panties down to her ankles, and then let them drop to the floor. Juice stepped forward. He put his left hand on the side of her neck, curled his fingertips around to the nape, and pressed his thumb on her ear. He used the fingertips of his other hand to roughly caress her clitoris in a rapid circular motion.

She squirmed. She gyrated her hips and her mouth stretched open. Several erotic moans sang from her throat in an euphonious falsetto. Her inner juices became outer juices, coating his fingers. He slipped one finger in, then two, and shook his thumb on her clit. Then, he lowered hishead to kiss and lick her clit. He parted her folds with his tongues.

The first delicious taste of her juices made him hungry for more. He fluctuated between sucking and licking her clit and exploring the depths of her silky folds with his tongue. "See what I needed from you?" he asked as he made a slow pass with the flat of his tongue, hoping to make her delirious with pleasure.

She spread her legs wider, granting him deeper access. "Yes, I see," she said and a heated moan tore from her throat.

He drew a quick breath and glanced up at her. His voice thinned to a whisper so low that it was barely audible. "Baby, you're dripping." Did she have any idea what that did to him?

A searing heat radiated from her seductive eyes when they met his. She whimpered and humped against his mouth. "You're the one who made it drip."

Juice pushed a finger in and swirled it around her liquid warmth. She grew slicker with each stroke. Her whole body trembled. He went back to sucking her clit. Seconds later she convulsed in is arms and tumbled into orgasm. Her pussy muscles undulated. Panting hard, she shuddered and gripped his head for support as a powerful orgasm tore through her. Her syrupy release dripped freely over his ravenous mouth. He lapped at her milky sweet climax and held her tight as she rode every trembling wave of pleasure. A moment later her content-ed sigh filled the small room.

It was Juice's turn to unbuckle his belt and lower his pants. He did it quickly and his dick sprang free, already as hard and straight as a flagpole. So hard, in fact, that it ached a little. He moved forward and sank his erection deep in her slick hole. It was a pleasantly snug fit. Slowly, he began to pump his dick in and out. When he increased the tempo, he felt her body shiver inhis hands.

She took deep gulping breaths and rested the back of her head against the sink's mirror.God, she was so damn sexy. A low groan of longing crawled up his throat. He planted a kiss on her open mouth, pushing his pulsing phallus in her pretty pink sex so hard that she became frozen in place as if she had suddenly decided to try out for an x-rated mannequin challenge.

Two minutes later she became unfrozen. She griped his shoulders and cried out in heavenly bliss as he plunged into her. Her second powerful orgasm took him by surprise. It always amazed him how responsive she was. He let out a sharp breath as her sex muscles tightened and undulated around his dick. Gripping her hips, he angled her for a deeper thrust. He fucked her hard and fast, just the way she liked it, as he slipped his thumb down between their bodies and applied the perfect amount of pressure to her clitoris. Her sexy moan told him how much she liked it.

The depth of penetration and the feel of her creamy essence dripping over his dick sent him close to the edge. His breaths came in ragged bursts. She tipped her hips forward, forcing him in deeper. He thrust into her. In no time at all his slow strokes returned to fast, steady strokes.

She knocked off his skullcap and slid her fingers over his bald head. "So good....oh, it feels...so good," Bubbles murmured.

Together they established a rhythm with them both giving and taking at the same time. A low growl sounded deep in his throat as pressure began building inside of him. Perspiration broke out on his skin. He glanced at his reflection in the mirror and saw a man who was determined to please his woman.

"You big dick motherfucker," Bubbles whispered.

His gaze moved over her face. Her sweet brown eyes were clouded with love and desire. His heart twisted. Her high-pitched moans took his breath away. Sparks shot through his body as he gave himself over to his climax. Growling, he held her tight and stilled his movements as his dick throbbed and pulsed, filling her with his seeds.

Bubbles squeezed her sex muscles, milking him of his every last drop. She moved forward and kissed his cheek, his neck, and his lips.

"*That's* what I needed from you," he said and they kissed for a long time as his dick grew flaccid and slipped from her sex.

He realized then that the chief pilot's fascination with the jet paled in comparison to his own fascination with Bubbles.

King Rio

~Chapter 11~

They were on bar stools inside of a Hollywood joint on Vine, The Sassafras Saloon. The vibe was 1930s deep south. Wicker furniture, a lot of dark wood, and potted ferns like you'd find hanging on a Charleston veranda. It was 11:00 A.M. and the doors didn't officially open until 5:00 P.M., so except for the sounds that came with the staff doing what was necessary to prepare for that evening's crowd--a bucket of ice being dumped into a sink, the clinking of freshly cleaned glasses as they were returned to a shelf--the bar was quiet.

Blake had suggested they meet at the Sassafras. The manager had let them in early, saying it was the least he could do after all the time and money Blake had spent there shooting a TV commercial for Hennessy. This past summer the Grammy award winning music artist had signed a deal to be Hennessy's brand ambassador and creative director.

Dressed in floppy black sweat pants, t-shirt, sneakers, giant headphones, and dark sunglasses, Blake turned to the big guy that Bubbles had brought along with her. He pushed the 24-karat gold-plated *Beats by Dre* headphones down and around his neck. "So," Blake said, "you and Cup used to be real tight, huh?"

"Like brothers," the man who'd introduced himself as Juice said with a nod. "We grew up together on 15th and Trumbull. Best friend I ever had."

"He and I made a lot of money together."

"I know. I was in the joint when all that was going on, but I stayed in touch with him. Like I said, he was like my brother. I used to call him collect once or twice a week. He didn't really go into details. We couldn't say too much, you know, they record the calls on the prison phones. But, he told me enough. I knew he was in business with you."

Blake drank from the bottle of distilled water he'd stepped out of his sleek white RollsRoyce with, wondering if Juice knew that Cup had been behind the kidnapping and murder of Savaria's mother. Not that it mattered. He just wondered for the sake of wondering.

"You know what I brought you here for, right?" he asked. "Of course," Juice replied.

"How does ten apiece sound?"

Juice's brow wrinkled. "Ten thousand dollars?"

"Yeah. We're looking to do a thousand a month. I know it'll be hard to move that many shirts. I can point a lot of guys your way. Some real big-money niggas from all over theMidwest. Think you can handle it?"

"That's a whole lot to move in one month."

"If it takes more than a month then it takes more than a month. No biggie. I doubt it will, butif it does we'll be alright. No pressure, you know? It might take some time to get you to where Cup was. And trust me, there will be some setbacks. Just keep your hands clean and let your team do the work for you. The only things you should be touching is money and bitches." He took another swing of water and gave a sly grin. "Not that you need any bitches. You got the baddest chick in Chicago."

"Yeah...I love that girl."

"She's a real one," Blake said, thinking back to the times he'd shared with Bubbles. He'd loved her too. "But that's neither here nor there. Bottom line, we're about to get this money. You get that first thousand off for...let's say thirty apiece. That's twenty million dollars for you. There's a whole lot you can do with that kinda money. And just imagine if you can make that kinda money every month.

"Ain't no way I can imagine some shit like that."

"I know it sounds impossible, but it really ain't. It's actually very possible. I did it before. Cup did it for a while. The shit's really easy as long as you know how to keep your name from popping up in any indictments."

Juice nodded. He smelled like weed--good weed--and some kind of cologne. He looked like the kind of man who knew how to make a dollar out of fifteen cents--a natural-born hustler. He had a rose gold Rolex on his wrist and a nice-sized diamond and gold ring on the pinkie finger ofhis left hand. His demeanor was very boss-like: attentive, calm, not too talkative. *He would makea good business partner*, Blake decided.

"So, how soon before we get started?" Juice asked, grazing a thumb across the blacked out screen of his smartphone.

"As soon as you get back to Chicago. It's already there." Blake dug in his pocket and pulled out a white-framed Google Pixel smartphone. He slid it to Juice. "Just keep that phone with you. Turn it on when you make it back to Chicago. There's only one number saved in that phone. Callthe number and my guy will tell you where to meet him. He'll give you an address and a set of keys. You go to the house at that address and that's where you'll find the shirts. You can use the house all you want, but I suggest keeping it a secret. Let maybe one person who you *really* trust know about it. Nobody else. My guy will meet with you there whenever you're ready for anothermove."

"I need some kind of legit business to keep the law off my ass. I'm already doing too much as it is."

"I'll get you something. Give me a day or two."

"Aight. I'm with it." Juice extended a hand and Blake shook it. "One more thing, though,"he added, holding Blake's hand in a firm grip.

"What's that?"

Juice opened his mouth to say something. His tongue went to the roof of his mouth--perhapshe was getting ready to say a word that began with a D, a T, an N, or and L--and then his mouth closed and he shook his bald head, letting go of Blake's hand.

"Damn, what's up?" Blake furrowed his brows. "Speak your mind.""It ain't important."

"You sure? Seemed important a second ago."

"Yeah, I'm sure. It ain't shit." Juice scrubbed a hand across his face.

"Aight, man," Blake said in a leery tone. "Don't have me setting this shit up if you don'twanna do it."

"We're good. I'm ready to get this shit started. I want to…I *need* to see that twenty million.

That's the only thing that matters."

"What's up with them niggas you brought with you?" Blake's pilot had told him about the other two couples who'd accompanied Bubbles and Juice on his private jet.

"Just a few of my lil' homies. Some young niggas from the hood.""How long y'all plan on staying?"

"We gotta leave in the morning. You know Bubbles got a daughter. And it's Christmas weekend so we gotta make it back to be with the family."

"We got a concert tonight at the Staples Center. I'm per-forming. D-Boy and Deja, Young Meach, Biggs. Basically, the whole MBM gang will be in the building. Y'all can come backstageand kick it with us if you want to."

"I'll see if they wanna go."

Nodding his head, Blake stood up. Juice got up. They shook hands again and then departed from the Sassafras for their vehicles. Squinting against the beaming sunlight, Blake stared into the white GMC Yukon Denali XL that Juice had arrived in. It was parked at the curb behind his top-down Phantom Drophead Coupe. Bubbles was behind the wheel and the other two couples were in the second and third-row seats.

His driver, a stout little Mexican man named Jorge, had his door open and was waiting beside it.

A woman in the passenger's seat of a passing Toyota stuck her smartphone out of the window and screamed, "Bulletface! Mom, look! It's Bulletface!"

The blonde female driver of a blue Lexus SUV going in the opposite direction waved at him and said, "Please tell Alexus that Lisa Dorchester said she fucking *slays*!"

Blake grinned and offered a quick wave as he ducked into his Rolls Royce. His iPhone rang just as Jorge shut his door. It was Bubbles.

"My friends in here want a picture with you," she said.

"Sure, come on." He stepped back out onto the sidewalk and chuckled as two beautiful black women who looked like they might be sisters burst from the rented SUV and sprinted towards him.

"I'm Tirzah," said one of them. "And I'm Tamera," said the other.

"We're sisters," they said in unison as they both hugged him, one on his left side, the other on his right.

Bubbles came sauntering over moving a lot slower than the two sisters had, but smiling just as excitedly.

The three women were California ready in crop tops and shorts that left little to the imagination. Blake tried his best to keep his eyes on their faces and nowhere else because the woman in back of the white Mercedes Sprinter van on the other side of the street was his wife and he knew she was watching him like a hawk.

King Rio

~Chapter 12~

"Look at 'em," Jah snarled from the back seat. "Goddamn groupies."

"Can't believe I almost told him to stop calling her phone," Juice muttered, shaking his head. "Had to catch myself and remember what I was here for."

On the sidewalk ahead of them, the short Latino who'd held Bulletface's car door open was preparing to take a picture with a smartphone and the girls were all hugged up close to the rap star.

Jah gritted his teeth.

"That man ain't thinking about them," Rell said. "He's rich. Filthy rich."

Cantankerously, Jah moved forward to the edge of his seat. "I wouldn't even be mad if Tirzah cheated on me with that nigga. He can have that crazy bitch. I'll sign her right the fuck over. I'm divorcing her ass anyway, watch. I'm about to figure out how to do that shit in a way where I get to keep all my money. Then, I'm out the door. No, I take that back--*she's* out the door. It's *my* goddamn house and her ass gotta go."

Rell and Juice laughed, but Jah didn't find a goddamn thing funny so he remained cantankerous. He wanted to end his marriage to Tirzah as soon as possible. What had he been thinking getting married to the psycho bitch in the first place? It was all Rell's fault. If Rell's romantic ass hadn't proposed to Tamera Jah wouldn't have proposed to Tirzah.

"Rell, you's a stupid ass big brother, you know that?" Jah spat out abruptly.Rell and Juice laughed harder and louder.

"Man," Jah said, throwing himself back in his seat and scowling at his older brother. "Fuck you, Rell. I should punch you in your muthafuckin' ear."

More raucous laughter ensued. Rell had to wipe tears from his eyes. Juice went from slapping his knee and laughing to slapping the dashboard and laughing and then back to slapping his knee and laughing.

Jah's expression did not change. His face still tingled and burned in places though he'dspent more than an hour in the shower last night and another half an hour in the shower that morning.

"I thought they loved each other," Juice said.

"Big homie, you don't know what happened last night," Rell said. "She got his ass. Got him good too."

"What she do?" Juice was trying to control his laughter.

"She threw firecrackers in the bed with this nigga, then tased and maced him when he woke up. Funniest shit ever."

"I don't find shit funny about it," Jah said, but Rell and Juice laughed hysterically, the kind of knee-slapping laughter you'd find in the audience at a Kevin Hart show.

It was funny. Anyone could see that. It was sitcom shit if there had ever been sitcom shit. But, his eyes, although tear-less, were stinging as if they were full of poison ivy and he refused to laugh at his own misery. He glanced out of his window. His wife, her sister, and Juice's fine- ass girlfriend were walking back to the Denali smiling suggestively and throwing their hips like atrio of goddamn groupies. Bulletface was in his top-down Rolls Royce being driven away by his driver--goddamn billionaire.

Jah was so angry at everyone else that he tried to find something to be mad at Bulletface about, but of course he couldn't succeed in doing that. No real street nigga could hate on Bulletface. He not only had the baddest bitch in the game, the best album of the year, the hottest music artists in hip hop signed to his record label, and a net worth of $1.7 billion (Jah had goggled it on the way there), but Blake "Bulletface" King was also a gangster; a savage. A lot of Bulletface's enemies were dead and gone and it was no secret who was ultimately responsiblefor their deaths. Bulletface was a real nigga who'd risen from poverty to the very highest levels of success. Who could hate on that?

The girls were full of joy when they returned to their seats. Tirzah was so happy that Jah seriously contemplated smacking the smile off her face.

"He invited us to his concert tonight!" Tirzah said, bouncing up and down next to Jah.

"He had his driver take a picture of us with *his* phone!" Tamera said. "He's gonna post it on his IG page!"

Juice turned in his seat and looked from Rell to Jah. "Yeah, I almost forgot. He invited us too." The fat-bellied fucker was still laughing, though not nearly as hard as he had a moment earlier.

Bubbles shifted into drive and made a u-turn. She drove like a goddamn maniac, as if posted speed limits were merely suggestions and less than ten minutes later they were back at the Four Seasons. All three of their suites were on the top floor. The lady behind the desk in the lobby hadgiven an envelope to Bubbles when they first arrived at the hotel. There was a black American Express card inside and Bubbles had used it to get a suite for Rell and Tamera and another forJah and Tirzah.

The girls disappeared into Bubbles and Juice's room. Jah trailed Juice and Rell into Rell andTamera's room. The three of them sat down on the rich leather sofa and rolled blunts. Being inside of such a richly furnished hotel suite lightened Jah's mood about as much as his mood wasgoing to lighten. He sat aback and listened to Rell and Juice.

"We're in the game now," Juice said, breaking apart a bud of Kush. "Bricks. I got that raw for the low. We can take over the city like Cup did."

"What's the low?" Rell asked."Fifteen racks apiece."

"Aw, that's it right there. That's definitely take-over-the-city prices. When can we get to the money? I mean, how long before the pack land?"

"It's already there. All we gotta do is sell the shit."

"Okay. I know some niggas. Some niggas in The Hundreds. Big Mo and Petey, some Stones. Them boys got big bread." Rell was nodding his head slowly and thoughtfully. "I know some Hobos--they got BDs, GDs, every gang really, all from the Robert Taylors. They got long money. I know about a hundred niggas out our way we can get some bricks off to. And shit, I'll grab ten of 'em myself. Have my lil' homies pump that shit for me. After the first three bricks that'll be all profit."

"Easy money," Juice said.

Lighting a blunt, Jah wondered how much Bulletface was really charging for the kilograms of cocaine. Surely Juice had added his own tax to that initial number. Juice was a legendary hustler, the father to two sexy ass daughters who were always dressed in the very best clothes and shoes that money could buy; no way was he going to miss out on any free money.

"I swear," Rell said, "I knew that nigga Bulletface was really still in the streets. He raps about sellin' dope too much to not be sellin' dope."

"I had that feeling too."

"We're about to be rich."

"In no time," Juice said with an admirable lack of hesitation. "I always told myself that if I was ever to get a real solid cartel plug, I'd put my all into getting as much money as I could possibly get. Fuck the feds, you feel me?" He looked at Rell and this time there *was* hesitation. "But we got to be *real* careful. Can't let *nobody* know it's us who got this shit." Another pause. "We never discuss who the plug is with anybody. Not even our girls. I really hate that Bubbles already knows, but she won't tell anybody."

"Tamera and Tirzah don't know much," Rell said. "They just think we're tag-alongs…that Bulletface wanted to meet you out of respect because of the relationship he had with Cup. Everybody knows him and Cup were close friends. I wouldn't dare tell Tamera or Tirzah about any extra money we making anyway. They'd have their hands out in a second."

Juice chuckled. "The words of a man who has truly had his pockets raided." He sighed. "It's gonna be hard, man. Getting rid of so much product in the city when we got so many people getting shot every day. That gang-banging shit will have the feds on bullshit for no reason."

"Then we'll leave the city. I mean, we are Travelers, right? We'll travel. All over the Midwest in places where niggas put money over everything. I know a lot of places we could go to find a bunch of dope boys. We ain't gotta tell nobody that it's us who got the work. As long as they buy the shit, we can get rich."

"They'll have to do a whole lot of buying," Juice said, "because we got a thousand bricks to get off."

"*A thousand bricks?*" Rell and Jah repeated in complete unison.

King Rio

~Chapter 13~

Blake turned the television volume all the way up and didn't turn it down because they were on the verge of an argument and he didn't want it to happen. He was desperate for it not to happen. The Beyonce video playing on the TV was a much better option, especially with the way Serena Williams was dancing around Queen Bey's armchair.

Alexus said something."What?" he shouted.

"Don't you *what* me! Turn it down!"

He clenched his teeth against what might have come through his mouth and reluctantly helowered the volume.

Alexus was fanning herself with a concert flyer even though the luxury Mercedes Sprintervan was air-conditioned. "Why'd you put your arms around them anyway?"

"Because we took a picture."

She gave him a cold, neutral look. "Yes, Blake. I know you all took a picture, Blake. But why did you *touch* them?"

"Because they were fans of mine who wanted a picture with me and I didn't want to treat them like they might have some kind of communicable disease."

"Well, how nice of you. How very fucking nice of you, Blake. I bet those fans of yours were quite pleased to be all wrapped up in the arms of the famous Blake King."

The Sprinter was essentially a living room on wheels. There was a large television over a glass-doored mini fridge, eight impossibly soft leather seats, and tables for meals or laptop computers (at least that's what Blake and Alexus used them for). Blake was gripping the TV remote so hard that he thought it might break. He decided he was holding it that tightly becauseif he loosened up that remote might just fly off and hit the Mexican drug cartel boss right in the chops. *We're not about to start arguing over Bubbles again,* he told himself. *No. We're past all that bullshit we went through last year.*

"Alexus," he said carefully. "The only reason I even saw that woman today was because you want your product on the streets of Chicago. That's the only reason. I just met with a complete stranger to help you. Then--"

"You're so full of shit!" Alexus said hotly. "You didn't have any reason for still having her number saved in your phone to begin--"

"Then when I walked out of that meeting with a stranger, I found out that the girls he came with were fans of my music," he continued on. "And you know what fans like to do when they see their favorite celebrities in public?"

"Sometimes I wonder how I ever wound up married to you.""By saying two little words."

She stared at him for a moment, tight-lipped, and then picked up her iPhone. She thumbed through it savagely.

It *had* been a mistake slipping an arm around Bubbles, Blake thought morosely. It was a shame too because up until then they had been doing pretty well, treating each other almost like human beings. It had sometimes seemed that being together every day, ostensibly to raise the children in a stable home but actually a last-ditch attempt to patch up their marriage and discourage infidelity, was going to work. But, since he'd left the comfort of his Rolls Royce for the Sprinter, it had been bad. How bad? Well, terrible, horrible, no good, very bad actually.

"You uploaded that pic to your Instagram page, right?"
"Right"

"And you're going to be on *TMZ Live* an hour from now," she said. "Now I know they're supposedly interested in talking with you about T-Walk and about Deja and D-Boy's new album, but don't you think they'll want to know what the hell you were doing standing outside in the middle of Hollywood snapping pictures with your ex? Hmmm? Or did that not cross yourmind?"

He took his eyes off of the TV to look at her. "I'm tired of this already, Alexus. As far asI'm concerned, you could've stayed your ass at home if this was what you wanted to do today. You watched every second of me interacting with that girl. Not once did I do anything wrong. Not once. So, take that bullshit somewhere else."

She had faced forward again, her expression stonily set. It suddenly turned to a conniving little smirk and she nodded her head slowly and deliberately. "Okay," she said. "Yeah?" And then, "Okay." She began to maneuver her thumb across her smartphone, texting.

The Sprinter was floating down Rodeo Drive, two long white Escalades leading the way andtwo more at the rear of the million-dollar van. There were important people in two of those Cadillac SUVS. One was occupied by the team of professionals that usually accompanied Blake to and from business meetings and other music-related affairs. The other was filled with Alexus' 'glam-squad' - two hair stylists, a makeup artist, a personal stylist - and attorneys Britney Bostic and Nikkia Staples, two of the most sought after African-American lawyers in the country. The other two SUVS were crammed full of armed bodyguards.

Blake could tell by the look on his wife's face that she was up to something, but he didn't care to know what it was. His mind was on tonight's sold out concert. It would be his first time performing in six months and the only reason he was doing it was because the show was the last stop of Deja and D-Boy's "Trap the World" tour. With the two rap artists being his record label'stop earners this year, he wanted their tour to end with a blast.

He glanced over at Alexus. "Baby?""Don't talk to me."

"Baby," he repeated.

"I hope you know that I"m not taking my anger out on your side bitches like I did before.

You start playing those games again, it's going to be *you* who pays the price. Mark my words." "So now I got a side bitch?"

"Shut the fuck up talking to me, Blake."

He shut the fuck up talking to her and watched music videos until they arrived at her mom's Calabasas mansion thirty minutes later. She got out and went inside. He stayed in the Sprinter and waited with his iPhone in hand for the Skype call from TMZ.

~ ~ ~

"...and who better to ask about the whole T-Walk controversy than the man who was perhaps T-Walk's biggest rival? We've got Bulletface live via Skype. Bulletface, how are ya'?"

"I'm good, I'm good."

"Well, thanks for joining us," Harvey said. "First off, I wanna congratulate you for all your success in the music business this year. *The White Album* sold more than eleven million copies. Young Meach's *Live From Hell* mix-tape went platinum. Biggs's *Bar None* album went platinum. MBM has become an all-star lineup of Hip-Hop royalty. With the bar set so high already, do you think it'll be harder for D-Boy and Deja to reach the same kind of success?"

"Absolutely not. They're still doing sold-out shows from their last mix-tape. As a matter-of- fact, their tour ends at the Staples Center and they'll be kicking off another tour two weeks after the album drops."

"Okay, now to the burning question that everyone's been

dying to ask you."Blake grinned. "What's that?"

"What do you have to say about T-Walk's...uhhhh...resurrection, so to speak?'

"I'm just as surprised as everybody is, to tell you the truth. I thought the craziest news this year was last month's election and then this happened." He chuckled a couple of times, flashing his diamond grin. "Wish him the best though. I ain't got nothin' against that man."

"We've been hearing from a lot of people who say they believe you may have been behind the T -Walk impersonator's murder."

"People are crazy. Only thing I'm behind is good music." "Has T-Walk tried reaching out to you or Alexus?"

"No. Not that I'm aware of. Like I said, I'm focused on this music. I'm all about MBM. If it ain't about MBM, it ain't nothing."

"One last thing," came the familiar voice of Van, TMZ's go-to black guy. The camera switched from Charles and Harvey to him just as he asked the question Blake had hoped would not come up. "How did you happen to run into your ex in Hollywood today? You posted a pic to Instagram a little over an hour ago of you and three *beautiful* women, one of whom was Bubbles,the girl you were seen with shortly before you and Alexus got back together last year. Now, you had to have known that this would set social media ablaze, which it has already done."

"I honestly thought nothing of it. I was out on business and happened to see Bubbles with two girls that were huge fans of mine. They wanted to take a picture with me, so we took a few pictures. That's all it was."

"Has Alexus seen the pic?""Yeah, she saw it."

"And she was *okay* with it?"

Blake was about to nod his head and reply when something

caught his eye on the right; a gaudy splash of white amid all the green of the mansion's side lawn as bright as sunlight. He turned his head and looked at the splash of white and saw that it was Alexus running across the healthy green grass in her flawless white Emilio Pucci dress holding her gold-plated Desert Eagle in both hands like a cop chasing down an armed suspect.

"You wanna talk pictures with bitches!" she bellowed. Then, she opened fire.

Blake was still live on *TMZ Live*.

The footage went viral within minutes.

~Chapter 14~

"Holy…fucking…shit," Tirzah murmured. "Daaamnnn," Jah said.

"What the fuck!" Rell called out.

"Hell to the naw," Tamera said, hands over her nose and mouth as if she was getting readyto sneeze.

The six of them were standing in front of the television in Bubbles and Juice's presidential suite, each of them wearing shocked expressions. Bubbles had phoned Juice and told him that Blake was about to be on *TMZ Live* after the commercial break. He had walked in with Jah and Rell just as Blake's face appeared on the screen. Now, they all stood with their eyes and mouths agape trying to digest what they'd just witnessed. All of their phones were ringing nonstop and Bulletface's Instagram post was obviously the reason.

"I'm not surprised at all," Bubbles said. "I've *been* telling people that that bitch was crazy.

Bet they'll believe me now."

"Oh my God," Tamera said. "What if she shot him? What if she *killed* him?"

Bubbles shook her head. "Suddenly I don't feel like staying even a single night here. Anybody else ready to get back on that plane? I have the pilot's phone number. We can be back in Chicago in two hours flat."

"Damn that," Tirzah said. "We just--"

"Yeah," Rell said, "let's get back to the city. We got money to make. I'm not tryna be all on TV, which is exactly what's about to happen if we stay here overnight. We need to get home. ASAP."

Tamera and Tirzah both turned to Rell and regarded him with nasty looks.

"He's right," Bubbles said. "And not just because of the cameras that'll be flashing in our faces everywhere we go. Alexus is pissed off. She's dangerous when she's happy...I can't even imagine how dangerous she is when she's pissed. I say we leave now."

All eyes went to Juice. Apparently, since he was the oldest in the room they were giving him the final say. He sat down on the sofa, thought for a long moment, and then said, "If we leave this hotel while it's still daytime we'll be on a million different Snapchats before we even make it to the airport. We'll leave out at one or two in the morning. Bubbles, check and see if we'll be able to get to the jet that late. If not, we'll get plane tickets."

"Okay." Bubbles nodded. She confirmed the late-night flight with Herbert.

The other two couples went into their own suites, leaving Bubbles and Juice alone. She stood in front of him with her hands on her hips thinking about what had just happened to the most famous rapper in the music industry. She wondered if he was wounded; if he was dead. She'd know soon enough. The police had to be on their way to...well, wherever Blake had been when the shots were fired.

Juice leaned back and looked up at her. He interlaced his thick fingers on his bald head and searched her eyes with his. She attempted to read his expression and failed. There was something in those eyes, something she didn't like.

"What?" she asked.

He tightened his lips and shook his head. It was barely even a shake, more like a bobble- head that was running low on bobbles.

Her phone rang again and when she saw it was her daughter calling this time she answered. Via FaceTime Ra'Mya's excited little face, virtually a replica of her mother's at that age, filled the screen.

"Ma, you're on TV!"

"I know that, Mya. How's everything going over there?"

"My sisters are about to do my *hair.*" She added twelve R's to the word. "I just got my nails done. We just ate pizza at the shop."

"So, you're having fun?"

Ra'Mya nodded enthusiastically. "*Tons* of fun. Everybody's talking about you and Bulletface now. Shawnna said she thinks Alexus is jealous of her daddy's *main thang.*" She laughed.

"I don't believe that's the case. She just doesn't trust him. He's done a lot in the past to make her not trust him, that's all it is." *Including sleeping with me when he was married to her*, Bubbles thought. "Listen, I want you to go online and find twenty-five more things you want for Christmas. Text me all the links."

"Can I make it gifts for some of my classmates? I think Juice already got me everything I wanted. Some of my friends need backpacks and shoes. One of my friends doesn't even have a coat to wear."

Bubbles smiled proudly and agreed to her daughter's request, though she still intended to use the black card to purchase some things for herself and Ra'Mya. She had already used it to buy the Gucci summer outfits Tamera, Tirzah, and she were wearing now and the Le Vian chocolate diamond earrings that were dangling from her lobes.

She ended the FaceTime call and her eyes returned to Juice's. Once again, she found that mysterious *something* lying dormant just behind his pupils. "What?" she asked again.

"Nothing." He moved his interlaced fingers to the swell of his belly, sank deeper into the sofa, and then let out a heavy nasal breath.

"Oh, it's something. I've been with you long enough to know when there's something bothering you."

"It ain't nothing. I'm thinking about how much money I'm about to make and hoping you didn't just fuck it all up over a picture."

She drew her head forward so that her chin rested on her chest. "So, it's *my* fault now? It's my fault that Blake's wife just shot at him?"

"Why would you take a picture with him in the first place? That was the stupidest move you could've made. And it was disrespectful."

"How? How was it disrespectful?"

"You know how it was disrespectful. You get all funny-faced if I even *mention* a bitch I used to fuck with. But, it's okay for you to let a nigga you used to fuck wrap his arm around you for a picture? It's cool, though. I ain't mad at the player or the game. My heart ain't broke. All I want is the kilos. Fuck a heartbreak."

She stared coldly at him for a moment. The potent aroma of weed seemed to radiate from hispores. His eyes never left hers, but she wished they would look elsewhere because right now she hated those eyes. The eyes she usually loved gazing into had suddenly become the eyes shehated. She thought of the story Tirzah had shared with her just before the boys walked in-- the story about her pepper-spraying Jah last night-- and she wished she had a can of pepper spray forJuice's eyes. That's how much she hated them right now.

She gave her own little bobble-head nod, only hers was up and down instead of left to right.

She turned, flipped him a middle finger, and then walked calmly to the bathroom. She shut the door, locked it, went to the sink, and then looked at herself in the mirror. "I'm not about to cry," she said as she began to cry.

~Chapter 15~

Jamal Cushenberry was on the record as being Chicago's 698th homicide victim of 2016 andthere had already been three more young black men killed and seventeen others wounded from gun violence across the city.

Homicide detectives J.W. Bryant and Roy Milam had the Cushenberry case. Neither of them had any hopes of ever solving it, but it wouldn't hurt to try. Besides, hadn't this last quarter ofthe year been overflowing with miracles? The Cubs had broken that 108-year curse and won the World Series. Trump would be in the White House in less than thirty days, finally breaking that 8-year nigger curse. Things couldn't be greater, in Bryant's opinion, and the idea that a third strike of luck might come in the form of a solved homicide didn't seem so far-fetched.

Bryant's matte-black Challenger had a way of dispersing groups of west-side gang memberswhenever they saw it, which was exactly what happened when he cruised around the corner from15[th] Street and onto Spaulding Avenue. There were five of them. They were gathered at the open

sliding-door of a red Chevy van just getting ready to climb in by the looks of it. Three of them

turned and walked off down the snow-covered sidewalk as Bryant and Milam-- two brawnywhite men who were real gym fanatics-- got out of the Challenger and approached the van. Milam ordered the remaining two young gangbangers to take a hike with their three friends while Bryant walked up to the van's driver-side door to get a look at the man they'd come for.

His name was Christopher Walsh--alias Styro--and his hands were open on top of the steering wheel. He was heavyset and dark with long dreadlocks pulled back in a ponytail. He wore a red Bulls jacket. The girl in the passenger seat was just as black as he was. Milam appeared at her window with his gun drawn.

"Out of the van," Bryant barked. "Both of you. Step out with your hands up and don't make any sudden moves." He drew his own Glock for good measure, pulled open the door, and the stepped aside as Styro got out. "Hands on the hood of the car. Got any weapons on you?"

"Y'all took all my weapons," Styro said. He walked to the Challenger with his hands in the crisp air giving Bryant a look that was as cold as the slush he was walking on. "Hope y'all know I got a lawsuit pending against y'all for that bogus ass raid y'all did on my girl's house early this month."

"Bogus?" Bryant chuckled. "We found heroin and coke, forty grand in cash, and AK-47, and a bunch of other guns. Nothing bogus about that."

Styro put his hands on the hood of the Challenger and leaned forward. His jaw muscles flexed as Bryant began the pat down.

"I'll tell you what's bogus," Bryant said. "What's bogus is what happened to Jamal Cushenberry over on Trumbull last night."

"What that got to do with me?"

"That's what I'm out here trying to find out."

"I don't even be over there," Styro said, barely moving his mouth while looking in every direction. "Is this even legal? Why am I being searched?"

"Suspicious activity," Bryant offered. "But pretty soon we won't even need a reason to search you. When Trump gets in office, guess what? Stop-and-frisk, that's what. Stop and fucking frisk. We'll need thirty more prisons to fit all of you gangbangers."

Searching through Styro's pockets, Bryant found a small bud of marijuana and placed it on the hood of his car so Styro could see it. "You're under arrest for possession of marijuana," Bryant said and then quickly handcuffed Styro.

"And possession of a firearm," Milam said as he raised a revolver he'd just retrieved from inside of the van.

Styro wasn't dumb enough to actually have a gun in his van after having just paid $35,000.00 cash to bond out of jail on drug and weapons charges. It was a set up. Milam had planted the gun.

"Y'all can't get away with this shit," Styro said, but his expression said he knew that they could. "All I know is the lil' nigga was makin' threats against Jah. He threatened to kill Jah over his sister gettin' jumped. That's all I know. On my son, that's all I know."

"Who's Jah?" Bryant asked. "I don't know his real name."

"Know where he lives? Where he works? Where he hangs out?""All I know is they call him Jah."

Nodding his head, Bryant removed the cuffs and gave Styro a pat on the back. The girl from the passenger's seat was scowling from across the street where she stood with her hip against the bumper of an old Tahoe that had been booted for unpaid tickets. Two children who had been throwing snowballs when Bryant round the corner were now standing behind the girl.

Without another word, Bryant and Milam got back in the Challenger and Bryant headed up Spaulding towards 16th Street. He slowed the car and lowered Milam's window as they came up on the five teenage boys who'd walked off from Styro's van. "Hey!" he shouted.

They looked at him.

"Your guy Styro's a snitch," Bryant said. "He just volunteered the name of Jamal Cushenberry's killer. Tell Jah we're looking for him." He pulled off, grinning wryly at the surprised expressions on their faces.

Milam closed the window and high-fived Bryant. "Fucking genius," he said."I give it twenty-four hours," Bryant told him.

"Twenty-four? I say twelve."

"Wonder who Jah is," Bryant said. "I haven't heard of him."

"Neither have I. We need to find Cushenberry's sister, see if we can get her to talk."

Bryant had spoken to the victim's mother, Larissa Burwyn, around three o'clock that morning. He'd delivered the news of her son's murder and listened to her spirit disintegrate while he sat at his desk drinking coffee with Jamal Cushenberry's criminal history pulled up on his computer. Starting at the age of twelve, Cushenberry had been arrested fourteen times, including twice for discharging a firearm, once for attempted murder, and three times for possession of loaded firearms. He was a documented gang member who, in Bryant's opinion, had deserved every bullet his nappy little head had taken. One less welfare baby for taxpayers to feedis how he saw it.

He picked up his cell phone and made another call to Larissa Burwyn.

~Chapter 16~

She was fresh out of the shower when the phone began to ring, but although the house was still full of relatives--she could hear them downstairs; it seemed they would never go away; it seemed like there were a hundred of them-- no one picked up. Nor did the answering machine as she had programmed it to do after the fifth ring.

Larissa went to the phone on the bedside table, wrapping herself in a bath towel with her wethair thwacking unpleasantly on the back of her neck and bare shoulders. She picked up the phone and said hello and then he said her name. It was the detective. His voice had been echoing through her head since three that morning and one word was all she needed.

For a moment, she couldn't speak or even breathe. He had caught her on the exhale and her lungs felt as flat as sheets of paper. Then, as he said her name again (sounding hesitant and unsure of himself), the strength slipped from her legs. They turned to limp noodles and she sat onthe bed, the towel falling off of her and her wet bottom dampening the sheet beneath her. If the bed hadn't been there she would have gone to the floor. Her teeth clicked together and thatstarted her breathing again.

"Is it James?" she asked, fearing the worst for her eighteen-year-old son; fearing that he might have gone out and got himself killed like Jamal had. "Is it *James? What happened?*" In hernormal voice this might have come out sounding shrewish--a mother scolding her bad-ass five- year-old for coloring on t he hallway walls yet again--but now it emerged in a kind of horrified growl. The murmuring relatives below her were, after all, planning her youngest son's funeral.

Detective Bryant made a noise. It was a bewildered sound.

"No, Ma'am. It's not about James. It's concerning the investigation into Jamal's passing. I just got word about a sister of his who was assaulted recently."

"Oh, yes." Larissa sighed. "Mila.""Mila's his sister?"

"Yes. I have four kids. Two girls and two boys: Jamal, James, Sherri, and Mila. Some people jumped Mila the other day...put her in the hospital. She just came home this morning."

"She didn't happen to mention the names of any of her attackers, did she?"

"Not that I can remember. I can ask her."

"Think you can get her to come in and give us a statement?"

"I can ask her," Larissa repeated, drying her hair with the towel. "I can ask her when she wakes up. She's on pain meds. Been sleeping on and off ever since she walked through thedoor."

"I'm in the neighborhood now," Bryant said. "I can stop by. Maybe it'd be easier that way."

"Sure. Come on over. Just give me twenty minutes--no, fifteen. To get myself together...to get dressed."

"Okay. See you in fifteen," Bryant said and disconnected the call.

Larissa sat there with the dead phone to her ear for a minute or more and then put it down onits charging base. She felt as if she was floating outside and slightly above her plump, damp middle-aged body, but she knew this was no dream. Jamal was gone.

Someone rapped briefly on the door and her brother called, "Larissa? Rissa?"

"Getting dressed!" she called back. Her voice almost cracked. She'd been crying all morningand she came very close to crying again. "One minute, please!"

114

"You okay?" he called through the door. "We thought we heard you talking. And Sherri thought she heard a thump."

"You nosy motherfuckers heard everything but this phone ringing," she said and then dabbed her hair again with the towel. "I'll be down in a few."

He chuckled once. "Okay. Take your time." He paused. "We're here for you." Then, he clumped away.

She lay back on the bed and cupped her hands over her nose and mouth, here eyes large and awash with tears that over-spilled down her cheeks and ran all the way to her ears.

She cried for quite a while then dressed and went downstairs to be with her relatives, who had come to share their grief with her. She found all the men--her brother, Philip and his two sons, Phillip Jr. and Josh, and her 18-year-old, James--sitting on the stairs that led down into the basement. They were loading handguns and passing a blunt around.

"A detective is coming over to talk with Mila," Larissa said. "You all better get going. And don't come back until whoever killed my son is dead."

King Rio

~Chapter 17~

It was breaking news on CNN: *Alexus Costilla arrested for firing gun at husband Bulletface.*

"Can you believe that?" Rell asked.

He was sitting upright at one end of the sofa while Tamera lay stretched out beside him with her bare feet on his lap. Her feet were well-oiled by now (he had started in on his New Year's Eve promise eight days early), but it was hard to focus on the foot massage with all the drama unfolding on the TV.

Tamera was watching it with him. "Ain't no way in hell I would be that pressed over a nigga if I had eighty *billion* dollars. Not million--*billion*. That's just fucking insane. And it's fucked up because the nigga didn't even do shit. He posed for a pic. Whoopty-fuckin'-do. You take pics with bitches all the time."

"Yeah, but we trust each other. Alexus and Bulletface are like Jah and Tirzah. Two crazy muhfuckas."

"Tirzah is off a little." Tamera laughed. "A *little*?" His brows rose.

"Okay, maybe a lot."

"Ain't no maybe to it. Your sister is fucked up in the head...and you ain't too far behind her."

"Don't fuck around and get kicked," she threatened.

Rell looked at her and smiled. He went back to massaging her pretty feet. His eyes traveled down from her juicy lips to her black-lace Victoria's Secret bra. Upon entering the room she'd insisted they both turn off the cell phones and strip down to their underwear. Rell could not have been more happy to follow her instructions. She'd packed on a good ten pounds or so over the past few months and all of it settled into the right places. She was thick like he liked her to be.

"Don't kick me," he said, lifting one of her feet to his mouth and kissing it just below the ankle. "I'm a lover, not a fighter."

She bit her bottom lip and grinned. "You're right, too. A lot of couples don't have the kind of love we have. Ours is a special kind of love. We don't argue. We don't fight. We don't cheat on each other. You're really a good man, Rell. I mean that. You're the man of my dreams, the man I prayed for."

"And vice versa," he said and kissed her other foot. "I wish we could teach Tirz and Jah how to love each other the right way."

"Seriously. Their relationship is toxic. They are like oil and water.""More like baking soda and vinegar."

"We need to do something to help them get to our level of happiness," Tamera said. "There has to be some way."

Rell thought about it for a minute. "I suppose we could talk them into going to counseling.

Marriage counseling or something like that.""Do you think Jah would go?"

"I don't know. You can never tell with him. He's too un-predictable. Won't hurt to try, though."

"We'll talk to them about it when we get home." Tamera rolled over on her stomach. "Massage my back. Enough talk about Jah and my sister. They're probably over there in their room fucking the brains out of each other and we're in here talking about them."

She didn't have to tell him twice. Her smooth chocolate humps were mountainous and enticingly soft, the recipients of at least seven or eight of those gained pounds. He poured some baby oil on the back of her thighs and slowly began to rub it in. As he inched his way up to her meaty buttocks his dick began to swell in his boxer shorts.

"You still owe me that carriage ride," she said, folding her arms beneath her chin. "Don't think I forgot about that. I'm holding you to it."

"I got a ride for yo' ass," Rell replied. With a beaming smile, he poured a crooked line of oil on her think derriere and set to work rubbing it in.

King Rio

~Chapter 18~

Room service at the Four Seasons was the greatest. Tirzah had just scarfed down a hearty 16-ounce steak with a baked potato and white rice. Curled up on the sofa with her iPhone in one hand and her second glass of red wine in the other, she was scrolling through Facebook laughing out loud every minute or so. People had already started making memes with the photo she'd taken with Bulletface, replacing his head with a crying Michael Jordan's or a nervous Pepe the Frog. Everybody was tagging Tirzah in the memes and she was having a blast reading them.

She was laughing at a particularly funny meme--Beyonce wearing a sly smile with the caption reading, *What, Alexus is in jail? I'm #1 again!*-- when her phone rang. It was her bestie Shawnna, Juice's daughter, calling.

"Bitch," Shawnna started, "did you see the post I just tagged you in? The one with the frog head on Bulletface?"

"Yeah, I saw it. I'm looking at these memes now.""You do know you're internet famous now, right?"

Of course she knew. In the last two hours, she had gained thousands of new Facebook and Instagram followers and her Snapchat following was doing even better.

"I hope not," she said. "I just wanted a picture with the nigga. None of us expected it to become such a big deal."

"I can't even lie," Shawnna said. "I'm jealous. I've wanted to meet Bulletface ever since the night we saw him in VIP the night Reese reopened The Visionary Lounge."

"We were just about to walk over there to say hi to him and Alexus when that nigga Darren got killed behind the club," Tirzah said, thinking back to that night in early September. The wine coursing through her bloodstream seemed to make the dream more vivid. "That nigga Bulletface was so damn fine that night. Mmmm!"

"Wasn't he though? Shit, but he's always been fine." Shawnna paused for a moment. "Money can make even the ugliest nigga turn handsome."

"He's never been ugly, Shawnna."

"I'm not talking about him. I'm talking about the no good bitch I'm four months pregnant

"I'm sorry to tell you this, but Bankroll Reese is also fine as hell."

"Fuck him!" Shawnna spat. "He's cheating on me. I *know* he's cheating on me. He won't admit it, but I know he's doing it."

"Join the club. Who's not getting cheated on these days? I told you what I just went through with Jah's nasty ass. You gotta take what comes with having a nigga like Reese. Being with him is like being with a...like being with a famous person. Cup left him a fifty million dollar empire and he's only nineteen years old. Take comfort in knowing your baby will be well taken care of. That's the most important thing."

"I know." Shawnna sucked her teeth. "That's what my sister keeps telling me.""Dawn ain't gon' give you no bad advice. Where she at anyway?"

"Out there doing my step-sister's hair. We're at the salon. I'm in my office bullshiting around on Facebook and giving my feet a rest."

"Tell that hoe I said hey."

"I will. What's up with you and Jah?"

"He's in bed. Taking a nap, I think. I ain't heard him say nothing in like thirty minutes." Tirzah swallowed the last of her wine and stared thoughtfully at the lip print her dark red lipstick had left on the rim of the crystal stem glass.

"Y'all still not talking?" Shawnna asked.

"Nope. I'm about to go in there and make him give me some dick though.""Ugh! After he fucked Mila?"

"I brought some condoms. You better believe I'm not that damn crazy."

Shawnna laughed. "Girl, go in there and give that boy some pussy. I'll talk to you later."

For a long moment, Tirzah sat there in silence, gazing at the ring that symbolized her marriage to Jahlil Owens. Would she be with him until they were both old and gray? She didn't think so. Not if he was going to be cheating on her.

She got up, wobbled on her Gucci heels, giggled at her failure to balance herself, and then walked to the bedroom. She realized that this was her first time being in a hotel room that had a bedroom. Usually, the bed was visible as soon as she walked in the room. Sometimes there were two beds. One time, back when she was still stripping at Redbone's Gentlemen's Club, she'd orchestrated an all-female orgy in one of those two-bed hotel rooms. Maybe that's the kind of action Jah needed to keep him from cheating. She was thinking it over as she made it to the bedroom doorway. Then, her mind went blank.

Jah was lying back on the bed with his dick out, stroking it savagely while watchingsomething on his iPhone. He looked at her, grinned briefly, and continued masturbating.

Tirzah crossed her arms over her chest. "Who are you on the phone with?" she askedthrough clenched teeth.

"Pornhub," he said without a moment's hesitation.

She walked alongside the bed and took a look at his phone. He hadn't lied. It was Pornhub. A big-bootied redbone was riding some guy on a couch. Tirzah shifted her eyes from the phone to Jah's face. Her expression changed from one of mild interest to one of pure disgust. She felt like he was cheating on her again.

She punched him hard. Her knuckled fist hit his right eye and by the time she was able to draw back her other fist for a swing he was out of the bed with his hand clamped around her throat. She landed the second punch on his jaw and then she was in the air, flying out of the door. She hit the floor hard and before she could get up he was standing over her. He gave her a sharp slap across the face that was hard enough to make white spots explode in front of her eyes. These spots shot around the room, drawing bright comet-like tails after them. Her head snapped to the side. Her hair flew against her cheek and she felt blood begin to flow into her mouth as her lowerlip burst. The inner lining had been deeply cut by her teeth; almost all the way through it feltlike.

"You think I'm some kinda bitch?" He was leaning over her, bellowing into her face.

"Bitch," she said and the word come out *bish* because her lower lip was swelling. She feltblood spilling down her chin in a small stream.

His fingers curled around her neck and suddenly she was flying through the air again.

~Chapter 19~

Juice heard a scream and a crash. When he stuck his head out of the door of his suite he saw Tamera running out of her and Rell's suite in her bra and panties. She was pounding on the door to Tirzah and Jah's room by the time Rell came out a moment later, pulling up a pair of jeans he seemed to have just stepped into.

There came another crash.

"*Tirzah!*" Tamera shouted, her voice frantic. "*Tirzah!* What the hell is going on in there?" She shook the door handle.

"Sounds like they're in there fighting," Juice said.

"*Y'all better not be in there fighting!*" Tamera screamed.

"Can't bring these niggas *no*where!" Rell muttered, shaking his head as he joined his wife at the door. "Jah! Open up this mutherfuckin' door!"

Something (a body, Juice figured), thudded hard against the inside of the door. Then, four seconds later the door swung inward and Tirzah came stumbling out into the hallway with blood pouring from her mouth and a cut on the left side of her forehead.

Juice's eyelids shot open.

Infuriated by her sister's battered condition, Tamera attempted to launch herself at Jah, who had just appeared in the doorway. But, Jah's fist sprung out before she could get her hands on him. His bony knuckles tapped her chin and weakened her knees causing her to fall to the carpeted floor next to her sister.

She turned to Rell as if it was him who'd thrown the punch. "You gon' stand there and let him hit me like that?"

Rell gave Jah a light one-handed shove to the chest and

then moved into the doorway with his back to Jah. At the same time, Bubbles shouldered past Juice and rushed to Tirzah's aid.Juice hadn't seen Bubbles ever since she stormed off and locked herself in the bathroom. He could tell from how red her eyes were that she'd been crying. She helped Tirzah up and then offered a hand to Tamera.

"Fuck all three of you punk-ass niggas," Tamera said, glancing from Juice to Rell and thento Jah.

Juice furrowed his brow. "How the fuck did I get involved? What I do?"

He didn't get an answer. Tamera and Bubbles helped Tirzah up the hall and through the doorwhich Rell had exited from behind Tamera a moment earlier. The door slammed shut and the men were left alone. Rell stepped out into the hallway.

"I didn't mean to hit sis," Jah said, pacing from side to side in the doorway. His teeth were clenched. The tattoos on his skinny arms rippled as the muscles beneath them twitched. "Tirzah got me fucked up, though. I don't know who the fuck she think I am. I ain't no fuckin' lame. Bitch ain't about to keep hittin' on me like I'm some kinda hoe-ass nigga. On my life, she got thegame all the way fucked up. I don't hit women, but I'll beat a bitch up if she think she can hit on me. I let shit slide last night. Not today, though. Not today." He shook his head for a long moment.

"What happened?" Rell asked.

Jah stopped pacing and looked at his brother. His right eye was swollen and his nose flared. "She *punched* me, bruh. In my goddamn eye." He pointed to the eye for emphasis. "I was layin' in the bed watchin' a porno on my phone, mindin' my goddamn business and she came in and punched me in my goddamn eye! I admit, I was jackin' off when she walked in, but what man you know *don't* jack off? And besides, I can do whatever the *fuck* I wanna do with my goddamn dick."

"Aw, hell no," Juice said and let out an entertained chuckle.

Rell went to the door of the suite and after two minutes of knocking and repeatedly begging,Bubbles opened the door and he was able to get his shirt and sneakers. Then, the three of them-- Juice, Jah, and Rell-- got on the elevator and rode it down to the lobby. Rell had suggested they go out for a walk to get some fresh air. Juice was with it. He needed to get away from Bubblesfor a while.

"I fucked up, didn't I?" Jah asked as they came out of the elevator."You never hit a woman," Juice said.

"She ain't a regular woman," Jah explained matter-of-factly. "Regular women don't taser and pepper spray their husbands. Regular women don't punch their husbands in the goddamn *eye*." He pointed at the eye again.

Juice glanced over and saw that Rell was now looking just as Jah had looked upstairs. Rell'sjaw muscles were flexing. He had his eyes directed straight ahead as if looking to either side might spell disaster.

"Let's not forget what the fuck we're here for," Juice said.

They were crossing the floor of the lobby. Up ahead, about ten feet inside of the doors, four college-age white girls were posing for a pic with someone.

"Once we get home we're in the big league," Juice went on. "Lucky for us, Alexus didn't even shoot Bulletface. I just saw it on CNN. They said she shot the van he was in, but it had bullet-resistant siding. As long as he's straight we should be good. We can't let what's going on with these girls fuck up our money. Me and Bubbles just had a lil' disagreement, but you know what I told her? I told her I just want the kilos, fuck the heartbreaks. I got kids to feed, properties to buy, millions to make. We can't lose fo--"

Juice lost focus before he could finish saying the word *fo-cus.*

The four blondes were scampering away from the person they'd taken a picture with and Juice was surprised to see that it was Alexus' famous lawyer friend, Nikkia Staples. She was a beautiful woman with a reddish-brown complexion and a sparkling white smile. She wore a form-fitting yellow dress, a big yellow shoulder bag, and towering yellow stiletto heels. Her hair was short and choppy with blonde highlights. One of the large, dark-suited gentlemen standing behind her was the same man Juice had seen inside of the saloon when he'd walked in with Bulletface. As he and the Owens brothers neared her, she locked eyes with him, squinted, and then spoke.

"Excuse me, sir. You wouldn't happen to be Juice, would you?"The bodyguard said. "Yeah, that's him. That's the guy."

Staples approached Juice, her stilettos click-clocking on the floor. She extended a hand. "Good evening. I'm Kia Staples."

Juice shook the woman's hand. "Nice to meet you," he said, his tone wavering withskepticism. "I know who you are. I saw you on TV a few times."

She nodded and got right to the point. "I'm sure you've seen the news. The media's about totear Alexus and Blake to shreds. They have her in jail, but she'll be out in an hour or so. Wewant to take control of the situation before the media can steer it off in a direction that might prove unfavorable to my client. I'd like to invite your girlfriend and her two friends out to dine with Alexus later this evening. And Blake would like for you and your friends to join him on his tour bus."

~Chapter 20~

Shawnna heard the creak of her office door opening. *I have got to get a lock for that door,* she thought. She was kicked back with her feet up on her desk, eyes shut, listening to 107.5 WGCI on her clock-radio. Rick Ross had just told her he thought he was Larry Hoover, a statement she greeted with some skepticism, and now the weather report was on. High winds were forecast and more snow was on the way; a traveler's advisory had been issued. There were apt to be visibility problems because of sheeting snow, per the disc jokey, but the thing to really be on the watch out for was the wind-chill. Shawnna knew what he was talking about becauseshe had felt it whipsawing the car when she went out to get lunch a few hours ago.

"Shawnna?" It was Ra'Mya's tiny voice. "Are you sleeping?""No, I'm up." But Shawnna kept her eyes shut.

The radio volume slowly faded to nothing. Shawnna thought of the *Rush Hour* scene where Chris Tucker told Jackie Chan to never touch a black man's radio. She pictured Ra'Mya's busy little fingers sliding across the radio's volume wheel and pictured herself slapping the back of the preteen's hand and telling her to never touch a black woman's radio, especially when the black woman was four months pregnant and trying not to think about the sneaky son-of-a-bitch whose baby was growing in her womb.

Ra'Mya said, "Okay, two things--no, three. Three things. Three things I have to say and thenI'll leave you alone. I'll save the best for last. The first thing is tea. Like, *really* good tea."

Shawnna chuckled. "You're not old enough to know about tea."

"Uhhh...I'm almost a teenager. Do I need to refresh your

memory?" She waited and then went on. "Anyway, when I was a little kid I actually *met* Bulletface. God can strike me down right now if I'm lying. He picked me up and everything. My mama got a picture of him holding me in his arms and she got another picture of me and his daughter riding in her pink Barbie Jeep. My friends at school didn't believe me until I showed them the pics. Now I'm the most popular girl in my grade this year, even more popular than Jessica Steinway and *all* the boys like Jessica Steinway."

"Really? Why is she so popular?'

"Because she let all the eighth-graders stick their little wee-wees in her mouth behind the bleachers."

Shawnna separated her eyelids and turned her head to look at the almost-teenager. Ra'Mya smiled at her.

"See," Ra'Mya said, "that's why you're pregnant now. You heard 'wee-wee' and woke right up. Steinway the sequel, I swear."

Shawnna laughed, picked up an empty Pepsi bottle, and threatened to assault Ra'Mya withit. Mya threw her head back and laughed, revealing a pink glob of chewing gun that was stuck to the roof of her mouth. Her hair was done; shiny black shoulder-length curls framed her pretty brown face.

"You lil' brat," Shawnna said, lowering the plastic bottle. "Gimme a piece of gum.""That's part of the third thing. Let me tell you the second thing first."

"Okay, fine. What's the second thing?"

"Do you think your dad is going to marry my mom?" "I don't know."

"I hope so. He really makes my mom happy and I think he's pretty cool. *Really* cool, actually. My mom said she's never felt as respected in a relationship. He treats her like a woman is supposed to be treated. I dig that about him. Plus, I've always wanted sisters and if he marries my mom that'll make you and Dawn my sisters and I think that would be pretty dope."

"You're already our sister," Shawnna said.

"Yeah, but not *legally*, you know what I mean? I want us to be sisters legally. That way you won't be able to disown me when you get used to me and see how annoying I can sometimesbe."

Shawnna yawned. "Okay. On to the third thing." "But I haven't even gotten to the second thing."

"Okay, *now* you're getting annoying. I thought the marriage thing was the second thing."

"That's why you get paid to do hair and not to think." Ra'Mya smirked triumphantly and pumped a fist in the air. "*Burn.*"

Shawnna snickered. "I'm not sure if you got the memo," she said, "but I'm actually the evil twin. Like, shockingly evil. *ISIS* evil. I once cut off a little girl's head for fucking with me whenI was pregnant."

"You can't scare me with that. It might've worked before I was almost thirteen, but not now.A few months ago, I watched a man with a bat wrapped in barbed-wire kill two of my favorite characters on *The Walking Dead*. Nothing can scare me now.

"Get to the third thing," Shawnna said and reunited her eyelids."The second thing," Ra'Mya corrected.

"The second thing," Shawnna echoed morosely.

"Is it true that you shot some girl named Big Wanda? I overheard a lady who was getting her hair done when I was getting mine done talking about it."

"Is this the second thing?" "No, it's a bonus question?" "Then I plead the fifth."

Ra'Mya sighed defeatedly. "Okay, okay." Another sigh. "There's this boy at my school. Helikes me or whatever and--"

"Don't trust him. Boys are liars." "He wants me to be his girlfriend." "Is he cute?"

"He's very cute. Cutest boy in seventh grade. Everybody's surprised that he likes me because I'm a sixth grader. Most of the seventh-grade boys go after eighth-grade girls, but Percy wants me for some reason."

"So what's the problem?" Shawnna asked.

"Well," Ra'Mya said, "he walked up to me as I was leaving out of science class. He pulled me to the side, asked me for my number, and I was smart enough to give it to him." She said it in a way that suggested her decision to give him her number might have been the opposite of smart. "So we started texting each other a few days ago. This was right before we left for Christmas break."

"Did you tell your mom about him?" "No," Ra'Mya said quickly.

"Why not?"

"Because I like having teeth to chew my gum with. Because I'm twelve and I don't want to die before my thirteenth birthday. Shall I keep going?"

Shawnna smiled. "Okay. So, you started texting him. Then what?" "He asked me to send him a picture."

Shawnna opened her eyes again. She brought her feet down to the floor, rolled forward in her chair, and fixed her gaze on Ra'Mya. "What kind of picture? And if the answer is 'nude' or anything close to it just hand me your phone."

Following a moment of silent reluctance, Ra'Mya put her iPhone on the desk and flicked it across to Shawnna, who instantly scooped it up and went to the text messages.

"I was actually going to show the messages to my mom when he started getting nasty, but she was already on the plane to California and I didn't want to ruin her trip," Ra'Mya said sheepishly.

Shawnna opened the thread of text messages that had been exchanged between Ra'Mya and Percy. What she saw made her blood boil. Not only had the boy requested a sexually explicit photo of Ra'Mya, but he'd also sent one of himself.

"Ahh yeah," Shawnna said, a cold smile playing around the corners of her mouth as she slid the phone back to Ra'Mya and picked up her own iPhone. "Text him and see if he can go out for a movie tonight. Tell him your big sister is taking you and you want him to come along as your date."

"Are you out of your mind?""Not at all, little sister."

"I'm not about to go on a *date* with him." Ra'Mya was incredulous. "I don't even want to goto the same *school* as him anymore."

"Trust your big sister just this one time. And come on with the third thing."

"Oh." The cheer returned to Ra'Mya's eyes. "The third thing. I wanted to know if youwould take me to the store to get some more gum. I'm all out."

Shawnna flipped the empty 20-ounce Pepsi bottle into the air. It sailed over the desk in a lowarc and bonked Ra'Mya on the head. Slipping on her coat, Shawnna shared a sinister laugh with the twelve-year-old. Then, they were out of the door.

King Rio

~Chapter 21~

Anger and frustration were two of the main ingredients in some of Blake's best music and there were large helpings of them in the freestyle he was laying down in the recording booth of his triple-black 45-foot-long Newell tour bus.

He had on his black and gold Versace robe, a bulletproof vest, black Balmain jeans held up around his waist by a black Gucci belt, black Louboutin sneakers, and ten million dollars worth of white diamond jewelry. He felt like his old self-- cold-hearted, calculating, hungry, unrelenting...dangerous.

Now I'm right back to that old shit / Bulletface on dummy, tape a nigga up like a mummy / put the choppa up against ya tummy / used to sell crack on Willard Ave / was a shooter then and

I still'll blast / Hit a nigga up, do 'em really bad / stack another billi, make 'em really mad...

He went on and on for seven minutes and forty-nine seconds. Somewhere along his flow he'd lost the robe and now it lay on the floor behind him. Four of his record label's music artits-- Will Scrill, Young Meach, Biggs, and D-Boy--were staring at him from the other side of the wall of glass. They were smoking blunts and sipping from Styrofoam cups of Fanta soda mixed with purple Actavis syrup.

Blake exited the booth and they all plopped down on the L-shaped black leather sofa across from the recording booth. He drank from his own Styrofoam cup and lit his own Kush-stuffed blunt.

"That was hard as fuck," D-Boy said. He was the newest MBM rap artist, a handsome light- skinned 21-year-old from the east side of Indianapolis. He was a dope boy, hence the name, who seemed to only know how to rap about selling drugs. "I wish I could just walk in the booth and go off the dome like that. On Vice Lord, bruh. That shit is unbelievable."

"It's because that nigga m-mad right now," Young Meach said and blurted out his peculiar life. He stuttered sometimes when in conversation, but never when he rapped. "Alexus got that nigga p-p-pissed off. That's that old Blake we just heard."

"I don't trust that nigga T-Walk being back in the picture," Blake said. "All this shit happening back to back got me feeling some type of way. I know Alexus don't trust me around Bubbles and I can't blame her for that. It's my fault for fucking with Bubbles from the beginning. But *shooting* at me, though? Right when this nigga T-Walk pops back up?"

Biggs nodded his head in agreement. He was another MBM rap artist whose name fit him perfectly; a hulk of a man who spent the majority of his free time in the gym building muscle. It was him who had helped whip Blake back into shape this past summer. "I see what you mean," he said. "You used to cheat on her with Bubbles, but she also cheated on you with T-Walk. Now that she knows he's not dead, she's overreacting over petty shit, pushing you away and leaving room for him to slide back in."

"Exactly," Blake said, gazing thoughtfully at the smoke twirling up from the end of his blunt. "That's exactly what the fuck I was thinking. The more I think about it, the more I see the pieces coming together. She did that shit on purpose. She thought it all out. She wasn't trying to shoot me. She knew the van was bulletproof. And she knew I was on *TMZ Live* right at the moment."

"On *The View*," Biggs said, "T-Walk said one of Alexus' lawyers had already cut him a check for ten million to help him get back on his feet. Some New York judge ruled in his favor. He won't be facing any charges. They claim he had the right to go into hiding if he feared for his life. The fact that the Rumsfeld guy was actually impersonating T-Walk when he was killed helped T-Walk's case a whole lot. They're saying he'll be on the cover of just about every newspaper and magazine for the next month or so."

"He better stay out of my way," Blake said. "On King Neal, I'll get back on that bullshit in aminute. It's been a whole year since I last shot a muhfucker. I'll do the shit myself. I got lawyer money. Fuck it."

"Big homie," Biggs said, picking up one of the five Glock pistols that lay on the table in front of them, "all you gotta do is give us the word and that shit is done."

"On the hood," D-Boy said and moved his head imperceptibly in something that looked like agreement. "My lil Post Road niggas can't wait to shoot somethin' up. That's all they do in my city anyway. Put a hundred thousand on his head and let the wolves eat."

Will Scrill was nodding, sipping, and puffing. He was that rare breed of rapper who'd made it big in the Midwest; A tall, antisocial kid who used his fists and handguns growing up in the gang-ridden Gary neighborhood he was from and his brains navigating the ego-driven world of the music industry. "The only difference," he was fond of saying, "is that in Gary they stab youin the front."

Will Scrill was strikingly handsome in his prime, but now, closing in on forty, he was fighting a losing battle with both his waistline and his hairline. But time had only improved his reputation. He was one of the acknowledged legends in the rap game and Blake was proud to have him on the team.

"Don't make any decisions just yet," Scrill said. "We don't wanna jump to conclusions.Let's wait it out. Right now the whole world is watching his every move and they're *always* watching you. Half the world knows that you and him never got along. If anything happens to him you'll be the first person they come looking for."

It was true. Blake and T-Walk's rivalry was well-documented. People were waiting for shit to pop off between the two of them. Blake hoped he wouldn't be forced to give the people what they wanted.

The Bulletface tour bus was parked next to the Deja and D-Boy tour bus in the parking garage at the Staples Center. The twelve SUVs parked all around the two tour buses were occupied mostly with Deja (D-Boy's girlfriend and rap partner) and D-Boy's family and friends, but there were also others-- gang members who came along in support of the other rap artists and a few girls the guys had invited to spice up the backstage after-party. Many of them were out of the SUVs, lingering near the tour buses with their phones in hand, dressed in their most noteworthy articles of clothing.

Blake checked his iPhone to see if Bostic had messaged him with an update on his wife's situation. No word yet, but he wasn't worried. Everybody knew Britney Bostic. She wasn't just a lawyer; she was the best of the best. Alexus would be home in time for dinner.

His cell phone rang suddenly. It was Nikkia Staples.

"We're pulling in a few spaces to the right of your tour bus now," she said. "Aight. I'm on my bus. Did you bring Juice and his guys or just him?"

"All three of them are with me. Their lady friends are in a limo en-route to L.A. County Jail. Alexus should be released within the next twenty minutes. She'll join the girls in the limo. There are all kinds of camera crews and paparazzi waiting outside the jail. Complete mayhem."

The other four rap artists introduced themselves to Juice and his two friends as they boarded the bus, then D-Boy, Scrill, and Biggs got off to mingle with their entourages while Meach went into the recording booth.

"Balmain gang in this bitch," Blake said as he noticed that all of them were wearing jeans by the same high-end designer. He shook hands with the three guys, forcing himself to grin lightly.

They all sat down on the sofa. There was a gold-plated box of pre-rolled blunts on the table.

Blake handed them each a blunt.

"Glad to see you're okay," Juice said with a slight grin. "I was worried about you for a minute there."

"I've been through worse." Blake let out a chuckle. It was a dry chuckle, forced like his grin. "My bad for putting your girls in this shit. I gotta take the blame. None of this would've happened if I hadn't called Bubbles."

"Don't feel bad," Jah said and removed his dark sunglasses. "You ain't the only one with a crazy-ass wife. Look at my goddamn eye."

Blake winced involuntarily as he took in the sight of Jah's right eye, which was bruised and grotesquely swollen.

"And that's not even the worst part," Jah continued, putting the shades back on. "Last night, the crazy bitch caught me sleepin' at *this*--"he pointed at thumb at Rell, who was leaning toward Juice as they both started laughing at something, "--nigga's house. She set off a pack of goddamn firecrackers on my pillow then tasered my goddamn ankle and pepper-sprayed me."

"*Whaaaat?*" Blake bellowed and immediately joined in on the laughter. He couldn't help it. This was the funniest thing he'd heard since his daughter told him about the African man she was certain Alexus was creeping around with. As a matter-of-fact, this took the cake. This was by far the funniest thing he'd heard all year.

So he laughed. He laughed until tears rolled down his face.

He laughed until his sides ached, until he had to put his Styrofoam cup down to keep from spilling it all over himself. He laughed until he had to stop to catch his breath before he could laugh again. Juice and Rell were laughing just as hard as he was, so he didn't feel too bad about it.

Jah nodded. "Welp," he said, "congratulations, Mr. Hennessy Commercial Man. You just knocked yourself off my list of favorite rappers."

After a while the laughter died down. Blake's cell phone vibrated with a text message alert. It was Alexus letting him know that she was out of jail. He read the message, but he didn't reply.He wasn't sure he what he wanted to say to her just yet.

There were eight or nine full bottles of Hennessy gathered under the table. He cracked one open for Juice and his boys, but he stuck to drinking Lean. A dense pall of weed smoke hungover their heads. For a moment, they were all focused on the glowing screens of their smartphones. It was Jah who looked up at Blake and shattered the silence.

"Apparently," he said, "I'm the biggest liar in the world right now. I just posted on my Facebook page that I'm sitting here on a tour bus with Bulletface. Everybody's calling me aliar."

"Go *live* on they ass," Blake said and quickly picked up his gun and tucked it behind his back. He put two more bottles of Hennessy on the table for show and he had good reason to do it. He had signed an unprecedented billion dollar deal-- $100 million a year over the next ten years-

- to represent the brand and he intended to collect every penny of that billion dollars.

He held up one of the bottles when Jah put the camera on him and said, "Henny gang over here! MBM gang! Shouts out to my Chiraq homie Jah! If y'all ain't got that new Deja and D-

Boy album yet go cop it! If you didn't get my latest album yet go cop that! Shout out to all my rap niggas in Chicago. G-Herbo, Lil Durk, Yeezy, Grindo, Sosa, Dreezy, Chance the Rapper, Sicko Mobb, King Louie, Katie Got Bandz, Twista…shit, I'm high so if I forgot to shout you out blame it on this loud pack. When y'all see my nigga Jah out in them streets show a real nigga the same love y'all give me. One hun'ed."

Jah turned the camera to himself and smiled broadly. "Now who's lyin'? Huh? I'll wait." He laughed and ended the video.

Ten minutes later they all headed into the stadium.

King Rio

~Chapter 22~

The sloppy-wet sounds Tamia's mouth made on Wayno's dick was the only sound made in the fire engine red Chevy Suburban as he drove down Douglas Boulevard. The snow was coming down hard now and the wind was whipping about even harder. It was terrible driving weather. He thought it unlikely that any enemies would be riding around looking for somebody to shoot. Even so, he had Lil Mark, a young hitter with a half a dozen murders to his name, posted in the backseat with an AR-15 on his lap.

As he turned onto Homan Avenue, straining to see through the blowing snow, he found himself thinking of what Lil Mark had told him a short while ago; that a cop had told Lil Mark and some other younger gang members that Styro had given up Jah's name as Jamal's killer. Then, a hard gust of wind tried to push him into the northbound lane and he concentrated on his driving.

They rode in silence for a while. Tamia, a cute-faced young short girl with a small waist anda huge ass like her older cousin Bubbles, sucked tightly and steadily. When Wayno glanced back he saw Lil Mark was lying back with his eyes closed-- maybe asleep, maybe dozing, maybe just pretending because he didn't want to talk. That was okay; Wayno didn't want to talk either. For one thing, he wanted to thoroughly enjoy the warm, wet blow-job Tamia was giving him. He hadn't had head this good in a long time. For another, just keeping the SUV in the right lane had become something of a challenge.

The snowstorm was intensifying. The road was a salted surface crossed at irregular intervals by white ribs of snow. These drifts were like speed-bumps and they forced Wayno to creep alongat no more than twenty miles an hour. He could live with that. At some point, however, the snow had spread more evenly across the road's surface, camouflaging it, and then Wayno had to drop down to fifteen miles per hour, navigating by the dim bounce-back of his headlights from the backs of other vehicles on the road.

It was almost 8:00 P.M. and the sky was pitch black. Every now and then an approaching car or truck would loom out of the blowing snow like a nightmarish creature with large glowing eyes. One of these, an old Pontiac Bonneville, was driving straight down the center of 16th Street.

Wayno hit the horn and squeezed right, feeling the suck of the salted snow against his tires and the suck of Tamia's mouth on his pulsing erection, as well as his lips peeling away from his teeth in a helpless snarl. Just as he became sure that the on-comer was going to force him off of the road, the Pontiac swerved back onto its own side just enough for Wayno to make it by. He thought he heard the metallic click of his bumper kissing off the Bonneville's rear end, but given the steady shriek of the wind, that was almost certainly his own imagination. He did catch just a glimpse of the driver--an old, bald-headed man sitting bolt-upright behind the wheel, peering into the blowing snow with a concentrated glare that was almost manic. Wayno shook a middle finger at him, but the old son-of-a-bitch did not so much as glance at him. *Probably didn't even realize I was there*, Wayno thought, *let alone how close he came to hitting me.*

For a few seconds he was very close to going off the road anyway. He could feel the snow sucking harder at the right-side wheels. He felt the SUV trying to slide. His instinct was to twist the wheel hard to the wheel hard to the left. Instead, he fed the SUV gas and only urged it in that direction, feeling sweat dampen his True Religion shirt at the armpits. At last the suck on the tires diminished and he began to feel in control of the Suburban again. Wayno blew his breathout in a long sigh and at the same time he blew his load into Tamia's tight mouth. She sucked out every drop and made a show of swallowing his cum as she sat up and engaged her seat belt.

"Man," Lil Mark said, "you's a good driver."

Wayno's attention had been so focused on the treacherous road he had forgotten his backseatpassenger and in his surprise he almost twisted the wheel all the way to the left, which would have put them in trouble again. He looked back and saw the dread-head kid watching him. His watchful eyes were unsettlingly bright; there was no sign of sleepiness in them.

"It was really just luck," Wayno said. "If I could say fuck it and pull over, I would…but I promised Shawnna I was on my way over there. She got a lil' problem she wants me to help her with. Some lil' nigga named Percy's been sending nasty messages to her stepsister."

He didn't mention that Percy was a 13-year-old horn-dog that he was going to threaten and physically assault when they got there.

"Need me to take care of it?" Lil Mark asked. "Nah, I got it," Wayno replied.

He wished Lil Mark wouldn't talk. He wanted to concentrate on his driving. Up ahead fog- lights loomed out of the murk like yellow ghosts. They were followed by a Dodge Ram with Indiana plates. The Suburban and the Ram crept past each other like great-grandmothers in a nursing home corridor. From the corner of his eye, Wayno saw Tamia moving around in her seat to some imaginary beat, flipping her long, silky-straight weave over to her right shoulder, recording a Snapchat video of her phone. She had a face like Zendaya and body like K. Michelle; a thick little bad bitch who was also a poor little broke bitch. She, like everyone else in the neighborhood, knew who the real hustlers in North Lawndale were, which was why she'd been trying to get with Wayno ever since he started pushing kilos for Juice. It was also why he had yet to give her a single coin of his hard-earned drug money...at least not until she gave him something *worth* his hard-earned drug money. Now that she had, he was going to give her a nice gift for Christmas. Not much. He had almost a hundred and ten thousand dollars saved up. He'd give her two hundred, three hundred at the most, and maybe she'd pay him back with two or three hundred more of those soul-snatching, toe-curling blow-jobs. Fair exchange.

He turned onto Drake Avenue and saw the exhaust fumes clouding up from behind Shawnna's new model Cadillac Escalade. As gray as the smoke billowing out of its rear-end, the Escalade had been a gift from the multimillionaire who'd planted his seed in Shawnna's belly. It was parked at the curb in front of her father's brownstone apartment building, which was brightly lit by Christmas lights that were strung up across the wrought-iron fence that surrounded it.

Wayno eased the Suburban to a stop next to the Escalade, threw the transmission into park, slipped into his thick leather Pelle coat, and raised the .9 mm Sig pistol from beneath his seat. It had a 30-round clip in it and green laser sighting.

"Sure you don't need me?" Lil Mark asked.

"I'm good," Wayno assured him. He pushed open his door, stepped out into the middle of the street, and then had to use both hands to push the door shut again. The wind howled around the Suburban, actually making it rock a little from side to side. He pulled the lapel of his coat over his mouth and nose and headed around the back of his SUV. The wind pulled his dreadlocks and the snow stung his face. He went to the Escalade's rear driver's side door and snatched it open.

Percy gasped. He was a scrawny little boy in a yellow coat, sitting next to Ra'Mya who smiled when she saw Wayno.

Shawnna looked back feigning surprise.

"It's my ex-boyfriend!" Ra'Mya screamed.

"Ex? I'm your ex now?" Wayno turned his attention to Percy. "You fuckin' with my girl,nigga?"

"No, I just know her from school, man! I don't even know her like that! I don't like her!" Percy said, talking at race-car speed.

Wayno saw that Percy didn't have on a seat belt. He grabbed Percy by the throat, dragged him out of the Escalade, slapped him across the face with the gun, and listened to the kid scream out in pain. He pinned the boy to the back of the Escalade, squeezed his throat, and pressed the barrel of the gun against his cheek. A sliver of blood ran down the side of Percy's face. He looked up at Wayno with wide, terrified eyes.

"You ready to die, bitch?" Wayno growled.

"Man, I swear to God I don't even *like* Mya," Percy cried.

"That's not what I asked you."

"Please, man--"

"You been textin' and callin' my girl, sending pics of your lil' dick and now you wanna cop pleas? Now you wanna lie? Lie to my mothafuckin' *face!*?"

"I'm sorry. I w-w-won't t-text her n-n-no more."

"Nah. Nah, fuck that." Wayno backed up, releasing his hold on Percy's neck, and aimed the gun at the boy's face. "Answer the question. Are you ready to fuckin' die?"

Percy's bladder let go all at once and in a rush. A patch of wetness appeared on the crotch of his jeans and spread rapidly down his left leg. He was full-on bawling now, really boo-hooing.

An expression of satisfied disgust momentarily tightened Wayno's face, yet he was also delighted. Some part of his mind wondered how he could hold two such conflicting emotions at the same time. He took another half-step back but the gun in his hand didn't waver.

"Nice," he said. "The cool kid who likes texting pics of his dick to twelve-year-olds can't hold his own piss. The nigga who wants my girlfriend just stood in front of me and pissed his pants. I can't believe this shit." He actually laughed one quick yip and then leaned forward, his dreads blowing in the wind like snakes that had hatched from his scalp. His vivid brown eyes stared into Percy's crying hazel ones. "I don't *want* to kill you, if that makes any sense. But, I also don't want you texting my girlfriend, so I really don't have a choice, do I? Do I? If I let you live tonight will you keep texting my girl? Give me an answer. *Now!*"

"I won't," Percy said immediately. Then, abruptly he dropped to his knees, squeezed his eyes shut, and clasped his hands together in prayer. "God, please don't let me die! I don't wanna die, God! I don't wanna die!"

Wayno left the kid where he was and ran back to the driver's door of his Suburban. The cold had numbed his lips and nose. He got behind the wheel and sat there, hunching his shoulders up around his ears, blowing warm breaths into the palms of his cupped hands, and then rubbing them together. Then, he dropped the transmission into drive, gave Shawnna a thumbs up, and pulled off. He drove past more homes shining with Christmas decorations, some blinking, some not blinking, some turned off altogether as if utilities had been sacrificed for the price of gifts.

"I watched that whole scene play out back there," Lil Mark said and then lit a cigarette. "Shit was *too* funny. Who the fuck was shorty? He couldn't have been from around here."

"You niggas are crazy," Tamia said. She was still on her smartphone, only now she was watching DJ Kaled's Snapchat stories. "I know it might seem like I never look up from this phone, but I do. I saw you snatch that boy up and slap him with that gun. What did he do to deserve that? I heard you say something about a step-sister. Only sister I know she has is Dawn, her twin."

"If you would've looked up from that phone for more than two seconds," Wayno said, "you would've saw that the step-sister is your little cousin."

He was back on 16th street. The Ram crept past again, followed by a rusty old Honda and then an equally rusted Buick. He'd seen some unfamiliar faces in the Ram; Black men, their eyes watchful. Were they enemies? Wayno wasn't sure. "You see them niggas in that Dodge truck?" he asked Lil Mark.

"Yeah, I saw 'em. Turn around and catch up with 'em. I'll let this choppa talk to 'em, since they wanna keep ridin' past like it's sweet out here." Lil Mark had the AR-15 cradled to his chestnow and he was staring out of the back window.

Wayno chuckled. "Can't just shoot somebody for driving past. So what's up, y'all crashing at my spot or what? I'm about to get out of this snow."

"I'm staying with you," Tamia said, but Wayno hardly heard it.

There had been an accident. It was just coming into view, about twenty feet ahead and to theright of the road. Tire tracks left the road at the corner of 16th Street and Spaulding, went ontothe sidewalk, and ended where the back of a large red van began. It had hit a parked car and then spun out of control, ending up half on the sidewalk and half in somebody's side yard. The hood had come unlatched and tendrils of steam from the breached radiator drifted out of the opening tomingle with the snowfall. As Wayno slowed the Suburban to a crawl, he saw a man come stumbling through knee-deep snow on the driver's side of the van; a big man in a red Bullsjacket.

When Wayno looked back at Lil Mark he saw that Lil

Mark was already looking at him, waiting for the okay to do what they both knew needed to be done. Wayno nodded. It was a split-second decision. There was no time to think it over because the big man in the red Bulls jacket was moving fast, waving one fat-fingered hand at the Suburban and shouting, "Aye! Wayno! Hold up! Hold up!"

Lil Mark lowered his window and showered the man with bullets. Blood danced in the air with snow and the man went down just as he made it to the sidewalk. Tamia threw herself onto Wayno and he thought he heard her repeatedly mumbling, "Oh my God, oh my God," but with the wind howling around the SUV and the AR-15 banging he couldn't be sure if it was really heror his imagination.

The man in the red Bulls jacket was Christopher Walsh, also known as Styro. He was gunned down for snitching on Jahlil Owens, who was better known as Jah, one of the most ruthless gang members in the city.

~Chapter 23~

Trintino Walkson strode confidently out onto the stage on the set of *Jimmy Kimmel Live!* Dressed in a finely-tailored blue Canali three-piece suit, he waved at the cheering, applauding crowd of smiling faces. He'd been here once before back when *People* magazine had named him "Sexiest Man Alive" a few years ago and to be honest he'd assumed that would be his first and last time gracing the stage. After all, he was only a TV producer with a few hit shows. His was a profession that required a lot of behind the scenes work. Being in front of the cameras had never been his thing.

But that was the past. Now he was a star. In the past forty-eight hours, he had been interviewed by every major talk show host in the country. The nation saw him as the heroic victim of a high-level conspiracy to assassinate a successful black man. Mainstream media was placing the blame on his feud with Blake "Bulletface" King, but the tabloids were suggesting a long list of varying conspiracy theories. He was okay with all of it. All that really mattered was the tens of millions, maybe hundreds of millions, he would make from selling the rights to his story. He already had a buyer, one who would undoubtedly pay whatever it took to keep the darkest pats of his story from ever seeing the light of day.

"T-Walk walks again!" Kimmel said and they shook hands as T-Walk sat down and gave thestudio audience another wave. "I must say, I've seen a lot of things, but this is the first time I've ever shaken hands with a dead man."

"It's an honor." T-Walk chuckled and put his on his most charming smile. "I'm glad to be here. I was just telling my friend backstage how much I was looking forward to this particular interview."

"You've had *a lot* of interviews today, haven't you? I flipped through my TV channels earlier and said, 'Oh my God'. CBS, NBC, ABC, CNN, Fox…it was literally all you all the time.Well, it was you all the time…until…you know."

The crowd laughed. Of course he knew. Everyone knew. Alexus had fired a gun at Blake on live fucking TV-- you had to live in a cave not to know about it.

"I don't know what you mean," T-Walk said, his voice be-traying the lie.

"Sure you do," Kimmel said, laughing. "A certain rap star and his billionaire wife got into a little on-air squabble, resulting in her being jailed for--"

"Oh. That. Yeah, I might have heard something about that." T-Walk reached up and adjusted his narrow blue tie. "It's an unfortunate situation for both of them. I've known Alexus and Blake for a long time. Their relationship is like that sometimes. I wish them the best."

"Have you gotten the chance to talk to Alexus since your return?"

"I have actually. Just for a minute or so. Her and Blake. They were both very supportive of my situation. That's why I said, you know, I wish them the best. We've been through some ups and some downs, but we've moved on from all that and now they have my back. I'm grateful for their support."

"Okay, now can you take us back to the day you found out you'd been assassinated in Miami, Florida?" Kimmel asked. "I mean, that had to be some pretty depressing news."

"It was, it was." T-Walk chuckled, but kept it brief out of respect for the Rumsfeld family. "Actually, it was quite scary. To have someone who's impersonating you be murdered because they looked like you? I don't scare easily, but that scared the hell out of me. That day changed me. I knew then that I was in real danger. I mean, here was a guy who'd gone as far as legally changing his name to Trintino Walkson, a guy who'd gotten all the same tattoos, a guy who'd studied my voice and the way I walked. I'd met the guy once or twice and I'm telling you, he was a T-Walk clone if there ever was one. So for him to be slain because of who he looked like...it was chilling."

"And that's what made you go into hiding?""Absolutely."

"What do you say to the Rumsfelds who are claiming you actually paid this guy to essentially become your body double because you knew that some bad people were after you? According to today's issue of The Wall Street Journal, the family is preparing to sue."

"That's a ridiculous accusation. I'd address it if it weren't a legal matter. My attorney advised me not to comment on it."

"Can you get into where the hell you've been since your funeral or is that also off limits?"T-Walk only laughed.

"So," Kimmel said, trying another angle, "was it warm where you were?"

"Sweltering. But that's all I'll say. I've been working on memoir detailing my adventures as a dead man in America. It'll tell everything. Should be out by March or April of next year."

"Did your parents know you were alive this entire time?"

T-Walk shook his head. "No. Nobody knew. Not even my brothers. That's one of my biggest regrets. I never got the chance to let them know I was okay. They were both shot and killed in Chicago. This was last summer. I talk about dealing with losing them in the book."

"Have you come up with a name for the book yet?" "T-Walk's Back."

The crowd applauded and a glorious smile stretched across T-Walk's handsome mulatto face. He loosened up his tie a bit. It had been a while since he'd last worn one; that snug-around-the-neck feeling would take some getting used to, but he was ready to start wearing them again. He was ready for the limelight and everything that came with it.

"And there you have it, ladies and gentleman," Kimmel said to his audience as he reached out to shake Trintino Walkson's hand again. "The most tweeted about man of the year has a book coming soon and its title says it all. <u>T-Walk's Back!</u>"

~ ~ ~

Ashley was at T-Walk's side as he emerged from the *Jimmy Kimmel Live* studio to a lightening storm of flashing cameras.

"Mr. Walkson! Mr. Walkson!" a chorus of reporters called out.

Holding Ashley's hand in a firm grip, T-Walk made a bee-line for the bone-white Rolls Royce Phantom they'd arrived in. It was a gift from Alexus, delivered last night to the gated Beverly Hills mansion where he was temporarily staying. A team of bodyguards cleared the way, muscling reporters aside as T-Walk first helped Ashley into the backseat and then slid in next to her.

He admired the fit of Ashley's sexy robin's egg blue dress as his driver pulled off. She had a very small waistline and a very thick ass and T-Walk loved every inch of her creamy dark Nigerian skin.

"Now they're gonna have *me* on *TMZ*," she complained, gazing down at her manicured fingernails. "Like Lawrence and I haven't gone through enough already."

"Forget about Lawrence. You broke off the engagement and you're staying with me now. You shouldn't even be thinking about him anymore." T-Walk kissed her on the cheek, put his hand on her leg an inch above the knee, and gave it a light squeeze. "I got us. Okay? There is nothing to be worried about. It's smooth sailing from here on out."

She turned her head and looked at him, a small grin playing around the corners of hermouth. "After watching you lie to Jimmy Kimmel back there," she said, "I don't think I'll ever believe another word that comes out of your mouth."

"What did I lie about?"

"You and Blake are cool now? You wish him the best?"

"Yeah...the best spot in hell," T-Walk said. "I might not like that guy, but I have to focus onwhat's important to us right now and that's getting this money and securing our son's future. I'mabout to get a movie deal out of this shit."

"But what about your friends who *died* because of him? What about Bookie and Craig? Andyour brothers? He had them *killed*, Trintino. They'd still be here if it wasn't for him."

"Let me handle this, okay?" T-Walk insisted. "You just sit there and look pretty."

He sat there thinking for a long moment. Ashley was a hundred percent right. In one way or another, Blake had manged to get a lot of T-Walk's closest associates murdered in the five years since their rivalry had begun. It bothered T-Walk that his many attempts at taking Blake's life had failed. He'd lost everything in the fight against Blake King and T-Walk hated losing. He hated it with a passion.

He scraped his thumb nail across the nail of his middle finger, the neurons in his brain steadily going off like car alarms after an earthquake and one of them zoomed in on Blake's most vulnerable weakness. "Alexus," he said and looked over at Ashley. "If I want to get back at Blake, I have to do it through Alexus...and I know the perfect way to do it."

King Rio

~Chapter 24~

The exhaust from the vehicles passing on Sunset smelled faintly of citrus. The citrus was lightly perfumed with exhaust and the sky overhead was as clear as a hard-shell Christian's conscience. It was one of those warm nights so L.A.-perfect that you kept expecting to see Ellen DeGeneres to walk in and announce that everyone was invited to take part in her show's *12 Daysof Giveaways.*

They were having dinner at Papi's, a five-star restaurant Alexus had opened earlier in the year. It was a celebrity hot-spot, a real star magnet that guaranteed an A-list sighting at least four or five times every night of the week. The ride there had been quiet. Alexus didn't want to talk and she didn't want to be cheered up. Brock seemed to know it and played soft music on the radio.

Britney Bostic ordered without consulting her--seafood. She thought she wasn't hungry, but when the food came she came to ravenously. When she looked up again her plate was empty andshe laughed nervously. The ladies--Britney, Bubbles, Tamera, and Tirzah--were watching her.

"I'm a pig, I know," Alexus said. "Didn't realize I was so hungry."

"For the record," Bubbles said, "I wasn't trying to get all up on your man. It might seem thatway from the picture, but I swear to God all it was a simple fan picture. My boyfriend saw the whole thing. He's just as pissed at me for taking the pic as you are with Blake. I admit it, it wasn't the smartest thing to do, but there was no ill-intent behind it. I apologize if it offended you."

Alexus nodded. "I appreciate the apology, but I didn't think either of you were in the wrong," she said. "If anybody's at fault here it's me. My dumb insecurities made me overreact and I messed up big time. *Big* time. One of those bullets could have ricocheted off the van, flown into the house, and hit either one of my children. Or if the bullet-resistant siding hadn't worked like it did, Blake could be...he could be..."

She broke down. A mental image of Blake lying dead in a casket brought out the tears. They surprised her with their fury. Half-expecting the paparazzi to pop out from beneath every table with their cameras flashing (and with the vast number of paps that routinely staked out the restaurant, it wasn't a far-fetched expectation), she lowered her head to keep her tear-streaked face from being blasted across the front of Holly-wood's gossip-mongering tabloids. She felt several consoling hands patting and rubbing her shoulders and the middle of her back, but that didn't stop or slow the flow of tears. She cried for five whole minutes, until her stomach hurt and her head ached. When the tears passed, she didn't feel better, but drained and empty.

And that was when Trintino Walkson said, "Alexus?"

She jerked around, her mouth falling open as she turned, knowing for certain that the voice she'd just heard didn't belong to who she *thought* it belonged to. But, it was definitely Trintino Walkson, sun-burned and strangely defenseless without his usual team of Gangster Disciples flanking him. He was wearing a sky-blue three-piece suit and a gold watch. He wasn't smiling and the fierce glitter on his sunglasses from the overhead lights made it impossible to see his eyes.

"T-Walk?" Alexus questioned tentatively, half convinced that this was some lobster-induced hallucination. "Is it really--"

"Yes, it's me."

"But, how--"

"The paparazzi gave you up. They were following me at first and then they turned around in their cars and sped off in the opposite direction, so I had my driver follow them. They're all standing around out front waiting on you to come out."

"Yeah and now they're going to think you and I are here on a dinner date.""I'll deny it."

"They'll still publish it. I've been dealing with them long enough to know how they work."

"So, let them publish it. Who cares what they think anyway? I just wanted to know if you're okay."

He moved his head, only a degree or so, but the light's glare slid off of his shades and she saw nothing but a calm, warm sympathy in his gaze. His tongue flicked out and moisturized his thin lips. He swallowed and his Adam's apple rose and fell.

"I'm...uhhh...I'm fine," Alexus said. *And you are fine as a motherfucker,* she thought.

"Okay," he said skeptically. "I don't want to wake up tomorrow and hear you've been admitted to some mental hospital like Kanye West."

"Don't even try me like that."

"I'm just saying..."

"And I'm just saying, don't try me like that." She smiled and her dinner guests giggled merrily. "Well, it was nice seeing you. Good to know you're alive and all, but as you can see we're having dinner here, so I'll catch up with you later."

"That's fine. Thank you for everything. I really appreciate all you've done for me these past couple of days. Can I get a hug before I go?"

She stood up without thinking, still shocked by the presence of a man she'd had murdered years prior. She had actually watched the assassination take place and the thought that maybe she had the wrong man killed had never crossed her mind.

The hug only lasted a second, a second and a half at the most, and then T-Walk departed with two burly bodyguards who'd been waiting for him near the front doors. Alexus sat back down in her chair hard, like a woman who had been unexpectedly punched. All eyes were on her. They were all looking at her intently and she understood some of the God-like power her celebrity friends like Mrs. Obama must have felt at moments like these, telling others what only she could know. And yet, she had to admit that it was a feeling she should not want to have too often. She believed the urge to repeat such a feeling would have corrupted most women--women with less iron in their souls than was possessed by the FLOTUS.

"I'm going to make him more famous than The Rock," Alexus said. "I'll own all the rightsto his life story, but I won't be greedy. I got him rich before and as long as he doesn't try to bite my hand I'll get him rich again. I'm expecting things to go smoothly. He's pretty smart. He's been about his money since before I even met him. I'll sign him on as one of MTN's top producers and reinstate his paychecks from the reality shows he helped create. He'll be back on top in no time."

"On top of *who*?" Tamera asked and then chuckled.

Alexus rolled her eyes, smiling. "Not *me*. That's for sure." But secretly she missed having him on top of her. He had been a gentle, passionate lover, the exact opposite of Blake's aggressive lovemaking.

In fact, T-Walk and Blake were different in just about every way. T-Walk was the refined, business-minded type that hardly ever stepped out without a suit and tie. Blake, on the other hand, was a devout street nigga who wore high-end t-shirts and jeans, iced out necklaces with blinging medallions, watches, and rings. T-Walk was the type of man you'd find in the boardroom at a Fortune 500 company, the type that enjoyed wine tasting, golfing, yachting, and traveling the world abroad.

Blake was more at home in a trap house, shooting dice and carrying guns with over-sized mags or in a strip club slinging cash into the air over some big-booty stripper. There were memes floating around social media comparing T-Walk and Blake to Drake and Meek Mill, mostly due to T-Walk's yellow-brownish complexion and his knack for wearing suits and mingling with the upper-echelon Hollywood crowd. Blake was dark-skinned and tatted from face to waist and he was friends with a lot of drug-dealers and gangbangers, the low-lifes, ifyou will.

"I saw the way you looked at him," Tamera persisted.

"Seriously," Tirzah added. "But who can blame you? That boy is as fine as they come." There was a Band-aid on one side of Tirzah's forehead and the corner of her lower lip looked puffy.

Alexus ignored the probing comments. "So, do you all want to go to the Deja and D-Boy concert? Pop up on your boyfriends?"

"I'm still taking in the reality of me sitting here with Queen A," Tirzah said. "This has to be a dream. I've been dreaming of this day forever. I have so many questions--well, I *had* so many questions. Now my brain's all tied up."

"I have a question," Tamera said and raised her hand half-way up before snatching it back down. She snickered. "The hell am I, an eighth grader?"

"Good question." Alexus smiled.

Tamera laughed again. "No, that wasn't my question," she said, stating the obvious. "You wear a lot of jewelry and you have even more followers on social media than Kim Kardashian. I was wondering if you ever worry about being robbed like she was in Paris."

"Me?" Alexus scoffed at the comparison. "You think Alexus Costilla is worried about being robbed? I'm the most powerful person on this fucking planet. Those robbers need to worry about*me*."

~Chapter 25~

Nineteen thousand devoted Deja and D-Boy fans filled the Staples Center to capacity. The beaming white lights on the backs of their smartphones lit up the stadium like nineteen thousand stars in the sky and it seemed like more than half of the crowd was smoking weed.

Rell and Jah actually were onstage with Deja, D-Boy, Bulletface, and the other MBM music artists as they performed "Flip a Brick", an MBM trap anthem that featured Deja and D-Boy, Bulletface, Lil Uzi Vert, and Gucci Mane. Rell was surprised when Uzi and Gucci came out to perform their verses, lending even more star power to the epic finale of D-Boy and Deja's North American tour.

Everybody had bottles of Hennessy in hand during that performance and when the song ended, Rell staggered off the stage with an arm around the nap of Jah's neck as Jah used Facebook Live to stream video of their once-in-a-lifetime experience to their friends and family back in Chicago.

When Rell saw their cousin Tara comment on the video, he said, "Love you, cuz. We T'd up for you and Kev. Tell Suwu I said solid, solid, solid, solid, solid..." And then he broke into some kind of made-up two-step dance because that's what he intended to do when he was intoxicated around his cousin Tara, her husband Kev, and her brother Brian, whose alias was Suwu.

They were heading back to Bulletface's dressing room. Rell hadn't seen Juice on the stage-- or maybe he had and just didn't remember--but now the big guy was right in front of them, chit- chatting with Bulletface and Biggs. There were a dozen young women walking with them, exotic dancers who had danced onstage during D-Boy and Bulletface's performance of their hit "Stripathon". Their presence made Rell a little nervous. He knew how his wife would react to him being around 'them bitches'--that's what she always called them--and with her already being pissed with him about Jah punching her on the chin, he didn't want to risk upsetting her even more.

So, he didn't go in the dressing room. He let go of Jah. He watched everyone mill into the room and then he reached in to pull the door shut and stood alone in the well-lit hallway with his back to the wall. "I can't believe this shit," he said aloud to himself. He was backstage at the Staples Center with some of the biggest names in Hip Hop. This was the kind of experience he should be sharing with--

"Rell," Tamara said in an urgent whisper.

He looked to his left and saw her. Three doors down from the door he was standing next to, his wife's head was sticking out into the hallway. She motioned for him to come to her, so he did, and when he got to her he smelled the liquor on her breath. She snatched him into the room--the sign on the door read Do Not Enter--and the same brawny black man he'd seen with the layer in the hotel lobby shut the door and stood in front of it with a second bodyguard.

There was a burgundy couch on the back wall. Alexus, Tirzah, and Bubbles were sitting on it with bottles of Patron in their hands. There was a chair at a small table that sat in front of a mirror with light bulbs all around it. This was on the wall to Rell's left and next to the chair was another burgundy couch.

"When did y'all get here?" he asked Tamera.

"Does it matter?" Tamera kissed him and he knew she was at least halfway drunk when her tongue entered his mouth. "I'm sorry I got mad at you earlier. You know how I can get sometimes."

"It's all good." He kissed her back, eyeing Alexus who had stood up and was now drinking big, face-twisting gulps from her Patron bottle while looking ravishing in a sheer white dress that hugged her mouth-watering curves, huge white diamonds glistening on her neck and wrists and dangling from her earlobes.

Christ, she was *beautiful*! And she was looking at Rell. Bubbles and Tirzah were also looking at him and they were smiling--wide, devilish little smiles.

What the hell were they smiling about? Why was there a crudely drawn sign on the door of this dressing room that said *Do Not Enter*?

Tamera grasped his wrist and led him to the empty couch. "You know how much I love you, right?" she asked as she sat down beside him.

"Awww shit," he said. "It's nothing bad, I swear."

"Never in the history of niggadom has something good followed that question, but go ahead."

All four of the girls laughed.

Tamera gave him a soft punch to the shoulder. "You're so stupid," she said. "No, but forreal, this is good. Like, *really* good."

"I'm listening."

"Remember what we said on our honeymoon? About the hall passes?" She made quotation marks with the first and second fingers of her hands. "Remember?"

Of course he remembered. He nodded, a smile burgeoning on his remarkably handsome face. *This can't be real. It can't be. Shit, here she comes!* His eyes widened as Alexus came over and sat on the other side of him. He turned up the Hennessy bottle and took two big swallows. Alexus put her hand on his knee, inspiring him to take a third gulp. The cognac played like a fire in his throat and warmed his insides.

"You wanna fuck me?" Alexus whispered in his ear.

"Let's have a threesome," Tamera whispered in his

other ear, rubbing her hand slowly across the chest of his black Balmain t-shirt and then down to the crotch of his black Balmain jeans. "Just me, you, and Alexus-fucking-Costilla. You down?"

Rell wanted to say yes--*God*, how he wanted to say yes-- but how could he after having spent the last couple of hours with Bulletface? On the other hand, how could he turn down sex with *Alexus-fucking-Costilla*?

"I see it like this," Alexus said, her mouth so close to his face that he could feel her breath on his cheek. "My husband has been cheating on me from the very start and I fell into the habit of taking it out on the other woman instead of him. But, on the way here, me and the ladies got to talking. Tirzah said we should fuck another nigga every time our husbands fuck another bitch. Blake is way up on me. If he can have fun, I should be able to have fun too."

"You shouldn't listen to Tirzah," Rell said and the girls laughed again. "She's not exactly the wisest person I know."

Tirzah raised a middle finger.

"Wait," Bubbles said. "Before y'all get started, Rell, I need you to call Juice and get him to come down here."

"Why can't you call him?" Rell asked.

"Because I don't want him telling Jah and Blake that we're down here."

Tamera started kissing on the right side of Rell's neck and her hand crept under his shirt to caress his abdomen. Alexus kissed the other side of his neck and began fumbling with his designer belt buckle.

He dialed Juice's number on his iPhone and listened to the ringing.

Juice picked up. "Man, where the fuck did you go?" The sound of LIl Yachty's "1 Night" blasted through the phone.

"Step out in the hall," Rell said. "What?"

"The hallway. Step out in the hallway. By yourself."

"Why?"

"Big homie, stop asking me all these goddamn questions and just do what I asked you to do. Get up right now and walk out into the hallway. And shut the door behind you. Trust me on this one. If anybody asks, just say you're going to the restroom and you'll be right back."

Four seconds later, Lil Yachty stopped shouting about why he couldn't have no wife. "I'm out here," Juice said.

"Okay, now turn left and go three doors down to the door that says 'Do Not Enter'.""What kinda shit you on, Rell?"

"It ain't me that's on it, Big Homie." Rell chuckled. "It's these crazy-ass girls. I didn't have nothing to do with it."

Bubbles pulled Juice into the room and flicked off the light switch, drenching the room in darkness.

Rell leaned forward and put the Hennessy bottle and his phone on the table. A part of him wanted to turn down the threesome out of respect for Bulletface, but that part of him wasn't very strong and it got even weaker when Alexus freed his erection and began to stroke it in her hands while Tamera pulled his pants and boxer shorts down to his ankles.

This was so wrong on so many levels, yet at the same time this was Rell's ultimate fantasy coming true. He'd always dreamed of fucking Alexus--what man hadn't dreamed and fantasized about fucking Alexus--but he'd never thought it would become a reality.

"Brock," Alexus said, "make sure that door is locked."

"Already did, Ma'am." It was the same voice that had said 'Yeah, that's him. That's the guy' in the Four Seasons hotel lobby.

"If Blake ever questions you or RJ about any of this, you both don't know what he's talkingabout."

"I don't know anything," Brock said.

"Me either," said the other bodyguard.

"Great," Alexus replied and Rell felt the breath of her word on his cheek again.

"Lay down," Tamera said. With her hands on his shoulders, she pulled him in her direction. She was naked and as soon as the back of his head met the seat of the couch, she planted her knees on either side of his head and brought her pussy down to his mouth. He began to lick and she rocked her hips.

Alexus straddled him, lowering herself gradually, and moaned as she felt him slide inside of her. It was one of the sweetest moans he'd ever heard. He thrust his pelvis upward and Alexus arched her back. The pace was slow at first, unhurried, but as they moved in perfect rhythm together, the speed became more rapid. She moaned again and he reached around and dug his fingers into the meaty flesh of her buttocks.

He couldn't help hearing Tirzah's moans coming from the other couch, but that was none of his business. *'Let me do me'*, Jah had said before carrying Mila off to the bedroom in their father's old apartment, so Rah was going to let Tirzah do her. After all, this wasn't *Cheaters*.

~Chapter 26~

Bubbles had peeled off her shorts and panties before they had even made it to the couch. Then, she'd grabbed his belt and quickly undid the button on his jeans while he whipped off his shirt and threw it to the floor.

She closed her fingers around the length of his thick, twelve-incher and began pumping it to life. "You want a threesome with me and Tirzah?" she'd whispered.

"Nah," he'd whispered back. "Why not?"

"Because she's married to my lil nigga. Y'all can do whatever together, but I won't touch her."

"It's okay," Tirzah had whispered. "I'll just watch."

That's when Juice turned Bubbles away from him, bent her over the couch, grabbed her hips from behind, and entered her hard.

"I'm sorry. I'm sorry, I'm sorry," she whispered with every thrust. "Shhh, shhh. It's okay. I'm not mad," he told her. "Fuck that picture."

He heard Tirzah moaning and as his eyes adjusted to the darkness he saw that she was fingering her pussy while watching him fuck Bubbles. No harm in that. If Jah were to bust into the room right then, he'd have no reason to be upset with Juice.

So Juice focused on fucking Bubbles. She threw that ass back, meeting him every thrust, and soon she was moaning like the other girls. Her tight vaginal walls gripped his dick like a set of pliers. She reached back with both hands and spread her thick butt cheeks apart. It was a beautiful sight, even in the dark. Holding her hips, Juice pounded in and out of her. He was relentless with his hard, rapid long strokes and he knew she wouldn't have it any other way.

They switched positions. She straddled him and he gripped her bouncing buttocks as she rode him. The rhythmic clap-clap-clap of skin hitting skin added a beat to her musical moans. Juice was vaguely aware of what was taking place on the other couch, but that was none of his business. Would he fuck Alexus Costilla if he had the opportunity to do so? Abso-fucking-lutely! No questions asked. In his opinion, Rell was the luckiest motherfucker on earth right now because if there was one woman that Juice found sexier than Lakita "Bubbles" Thomas, it was Alexus "Queen A" Costilla.

Bubbles told him she was coming and then his dick was coated with her cream. She moved to her knees between his parted legs and throated him until he shot off down her throat.

~ ~ ~

When everyone was dressed, Tamera flicked on the light and looked around at the smiling faces. "Okay," she said, "as far as the other two know we're all still pissed at each other. Let'snot forget that."

Alexus and Rell stood up.

She gave him a friendly hug and said, "It was nice meeting you, Rell." She turned to Tamera. "Let the boys leave out first. I'll text Blake in about fifteen minute and let him know we're here."

Rell had a smile on his face that he doubted would leave anytime soon. He picked up his Hennessy bottle, pocketed his iPhone, and both he and Juice kissed their ladies goodbye before stepping out into the hallway.

Juice stopped halfway to Bulletface's dressing room and looked at Rell. "You know I gotta ask," he said. "You ain't gotta tell me, but I definitely gotta ask."

The smile on Rell's face widened an inch in both direc-tions. In his best Future voice he said, "She got that billion dolla..." He laughed, Juice laughed, and they continued on toward Bulletface's dressing room. "You know I don't do no talkin' but even if I did niggas in the hood wouldn't believe me anyway."

"That's some amazing shit you just did, lil homie. That's the highest notch you could've hit.

"Man, I'm still shocked." "You's a lucky mothafucka." "I am. I know I am."

The conversation might have gone on for another moment or two if Bulletface's dressing room door hadn't swung open just as they were approaching it. Jah came out first, holding a bottle of Hennessy in each hand and he was followed out by the billionaire rap legend, Blake King.

Instinctively, Rell took a swig from the bottle to disguise the smell of pussy on his breath. "Where the fuck y'all been at?" Jah asked.

Behind him in the dressing room, Meach threw a tornado of cash in the air over seven or eight strippers who were showing off their exotic dancing skills. On the floor in front of the couch where Biggs and Scrill were sitting, two girls were sixty-nining.

Jah thrust a bottle at Juice. "You forgot your bottle. Almost had a stripper lips on it. You should thank me."

Chuckling, Juice took the bottle out of Jah's hand.

Bulletface sipped from a Styrofoam cup full of iced Lean. "Y'all ain't heard from the girls yet?" he asked.

"Nope," Rell said. "Nah," Juice answered.

"Fuck them hoes," Jah said and held out his bottle, which only had about two inches of cognac sloshing around inside of it. "Let's make a toast to the guys, man. Let's make a toast to the real niggas. I ain't about to sit here stressin' over no bitch when we got fifteen bad-ass strippers right here with us."

With another chuckle, Juice held his nearly-full bottle up to

Jah's nearly-empty one. Rell's bottle was almost half-full and he held it up to the other two. Bulletface offered up his Styrofoamfor the toast.

Jah said, "To all the gang members--Vice Lords, GDs, BDs, Stones, Breeds, Souls, Kings, Crips, Bloods...May we all keep bangin' til the world stop swangin', you feel me?"

"I gotta give my toast to the dope boys," Bulletface said. "Niggas that's out there trappin' right now as we speak. Niggas in the Feds for hustling to feed their families. Niggas sellinggrams and niggas moving bricks. Trap niggas all across the world. Let's get this money."

"Toast to all the fallen soldiers," Rell said. "Cup, Lil Cholly, Cicero Yaya, Ra-Ray, Wallace,Jaws, Junior, Lil Dave, and Head. The list goes on and on. May all my niggas rest easy. And maywe all keep God first and family second and get this money."

Juice nodded his head, sweeping his eyes around the circle. He said, "To kilograms and heartbreaks," and then they drank.

~Chapter 27~

"Mila Cushenberry?" Bryant questioned as he and Milam entered the living room behind Larissa Burwyn.

"That's me," Mila said and nodded her head gently. She was sitting at the left end of the couch near the front door that her mother had just led the detectives in through and she looked like she'd suffered through twelve rounds against Floyd Mayweather Jr.

Her left eye was completely swollen shut and there was a neat row of stitches beneath it. Herright eye was also swollen, though not as severely as the left one. Her nose had a peculiar twistto it and there was a vertical line of stitches alongside the left nostril. The right side of her face was twice the size of the the other side. There were more stitches where her left eyebrow should have been and in both sides of her upper lip. She had a multicolored quilt wrapped around her shoulders. With the partially closed right eye, she studied the detectives.

"I'm Detective Bryant and this is my partner, Detective Milam. Are you up to answering a few questions? We came by yesterday but you were pretty much out of it."

"I remember…a little."

"Okay. We're investigating your brother's murder and we have reason to believe it may be connected to what happened to you. Are you familiar with a man who goes by the name of Jah?"

Mila looked to her mother, who'd sat at the other end of the couch. Larissa looked even bigger sitting down. An ugly, jagged scar twisted its way down the side of her face and Bryant wondered if she'd soldiered through her own brutal beat-down in the past.

Larissa lit a cigarette and then returned Mila's stare.

"The hell is you lookin' at me for?

Answer the man," Larissa snapped.

"I know a few guys with that name," Mila said.

"Who attacked you?" Milam asked, lacing his fingers on top of his slightly overgrown crew cut. "We need to know. *Now!* Because if this Jah guy is the same one me and Detective Bryant were looking into last night, you might be in a lot more danger than you think."

Bryant produced a folded sheet of paper from inside of his peacoat. It was a six-man photo lineup. He showed it to Mila. "You see any Jahs you know on this page?"

She pointed. "I know him."

"That's Jahlil Owens," Detective Bryant said. "Yesterday we talked to a guy named Styro over on 15th and Spaulding. He told us that Jahlil Owens was more than likely your brother's killer."

"Styro with the red van?"

Bryant nodded. "Styro with the red van." "I know him. We used to mess around." "He's dead."

"Dead?" Her expression didn't change--couldn't change-- but she sucked in a gasp.

"He was murdered on 16th Street lat last night, more than likely because his girlfriend overheard him telling us about Jah's alleged involvement in your brother's murder and ran her mouth," Bryant stated. "When we were searching through our database trying to figure out which Jah might be our guy, we came across Jahlil Owens, a guy who has in recent years been name the suspect in seven other North Lawndale homicides. None of the charges can stick because everybody's terrified of this guy. We've yet to get a single eyewitness to come forward and point this fucking guy out. Now Jamal might very well be the eighth person to lose his life at the hands of

Jahlil Owens and unless you can help us out here, victim number nine could be coming very soon."

"Just take us through the attack from start to finish," Milam said, taking a notepad and an ink pen out of his breast pocket. "Try not to leave anything out."

The battered woman lowered her misshaped head. Her legs were pulled up under her. The smell of tobacco, old and new, clung to the living room's somber gray walls. The black plastic vertical blinds behind the couch where Mila and Larissa were sitting looked dusty and they were drawn shut. However, one rogue blind wasn't following the rules and it happened to be behind Mila, leaving her sitting in one lonely bar of sunlight. Bryant saw dust motes dancing in it. They seemed to give her a halo.

The house was cold and quiet. The only sounds were the low squeaks of the couch as Larissa leaned forward to ash out her cigarette and the low whine of the December wind outside.

Bryant glanced meaningfully at his watch. It was 11:24 A.M. Twelve hours and thirty-six minutes until Christmas.

"I was at the liquor store on Ogden," Mila said finally. "Me and one of my friends named Tamia. I was waiting in that long-ass line with her and all of a sudden I saw Jah and his brother coming out of the L. I said hi, Jah said hi back, we started talkin', blah, blah, blah, and he brought me over to that apartment building him and his brother got on Douglas and Homan. So we go upstairs." She raised a hand and stirred the dust-motes into liveliness around her head. "We're climbing the stairs and I all of a sudden had this strange feeling in my stomach. For one,

I remember hearing about one of the boys off 16th and Millard getting killed in that building when they was into it with Jah and his boys around this time last year. I think that might be where the funny feeling came from. Or it might have been because Jah got robbed and shot in that same stairwell. I don't know. But I felt it. I definitely felt something."

"So you went inside somebody's apartment?" Milam asked.

"Mmhmmm," Mila hummed. "On the top floor. I talked to his brother while he ran back out to the truck and when he came back up we went into the bedroom and--" she glanced at her mom, who was watching an Eddie Murphy movie on mute, then turned back to Bryant-- "we started doing stuff. And the next thing I know, his brother screamed for him to come and get his wife. He pushed me out the bedroom and his wife was right there in my face. See?"

She cocked her head to the side, revealing a nasty bruise a few inches beneath her left ear.

Bryant knew what had caused the bruise before she even said it.

"The bitch shocked me with a taser," Mila said. "That's the only reason them bitches was able to get me like this. I would've never lost if they didn't use a weapon." She fell silent, fuming. Steaming even. The dust motes and cigarette smoke twirled around her face. The sun made her guilt almost too dazzling to look at. It had a lot of bright-colored patches and it and some were even sequined and reflected in the sunlight.

"I lied at first," she said, after a time. "I said Jah was in on it…That's what I told James and Jamal, but Jah wasn't in on it. I was just mad that he didn't help. He didn't even try to help me, just closed the bedroom door and hid in there while those bitches jumped me."

"Those bitches got names?" Bryant asked and Larissa laughed.

"No," Mila said. "I ain't no snitch. I've said all I'm gonna say and the only reason I said this much is because of my brothers.

She fell silent again and the living room belonged to the sun and the dancing motes. Bryant gestured with a short jerk of his head and Milam followed him back to the door. He told Larissa Burwyn he'd be in touch as they headed out of the door.

God wasn't seasoning the land with his snow shaker this morning, but there was plenty of stuff on the ground. Every minute or so a gentle wind blew snow across the streets. A black Dodge Ram with Indiana plates rolled past as the two detectives were getting in the blacked-out Challenger and Bryant stared after it until it made a right turn on the next block and disappeared from view.

"Same truck that pulled off from here as we were pulling up yesterday," Milam said, engaging his seat belt.

"And today," Bryant said. "It was rounding that same corner.""Wanna tail it?"

"Nah. Probably just some drug-dealer the mom's dating. We've got enough on our plates. We need to get Jah off the streets. I want this case closed before the new year comes rolling in."

"Bud," Roy Milam said and placed a hand on Bryant's shoulder. "You're losing focus. Guys like Jah keep us in business and he's only doing what we *want* to do to these black fucks. Am I right?"

Bryant dropped the transmission into drive, glanced at the side-view mirror, and pulled off. "You're right," he said.

"I know I'm right. Jah's doing his part to make America great again and by God I say we lethim keep at it. Let's try and get the Chris Walsh murder solved. That one should be a piece of cake. His killer has to be one of those young guys and it ought to be easy getting one of them to talk."

"Those young punks are born-and-bred gangbangers. They wouldn't snitch on an enemy, let alone on one of their own."

"Who cares if they don't?" Milam was obviously in the Christmas spirit. His pale white face, red at the cheeks from the cold, held one big smile. "What do you say we head over to my place for a beer and a burger? Knock one back for old Trump and talk about how goddamn great it feels to be white men in America!"

Not a bad idea, Bryant thought. *Not a bad idea at all.*

~Chapter 28~

Everything had gone down just as Blake "Bulletface" King said it would. When Juice dialed the number in the phone that Blake had given him, a guy answered and asked him to come to a Brighton Park gas station--the GoLo on 35th and California.

The guy was about Blake's age with a long, lean body, short hair, and a very light complexion. He had been sitting in the driver's seat of a gray Maserati when Juice pulled up next to him. He'd gotten out of the car, reached in through Bubble's window, and handed Juice a set of keys.

"They call me Fly," he'd said. "I'm about to text you the address snow, but you can really Google it yourself. It's the old Michael Jordan mansion out there in Highland Park. You got a hundred boxes in the garage, ten big girls in each one. Hit my line if you need anything else."

Juice had arrived at the Highland Park mansion thirty minutes later. Bubbles had dozed off in the passenger's seat by then, tired from having stayed up with him from the time they left the

L.A. concert to the time they boarded the flight back to Chicago. Juice found the hundred cardboard boxes stacked in the otherwise empty garage. After checking one of the boxes to make sure it had ten bricks of cocaine inside of it, he'd put two boxes in the back seat of his F-Pace and drove home where he and Bubbles received a warm welcome from Ra'Mya and the twins.

Now, it was five minutes past noon. Bubbles was asleep in bed where she'd been for the past five hours. Juice had gotten out of bed forty-five minutes ago. He showered and dressed in a heavy tan-colored Ralph Lauren hoodie and sweatpants with matching Timberland boots. He topped it off with a skullcap and then went to his closet (quietly, so as not to awaken Bubbles) to get his Glock 23. He put the gun on his hip, sat in the middle of his big leather living room sofa, and sent out three text messages to Wayno, Rell, and Jah. Then, he watched ESPN while he waited for them to show up.

Wayno was the first to arrive. He sat on the other sofa and let out a roaring yawn. "Fucked the shit out of your girl's cousin last night," he said.

"Who? Tamia?" Juice asked.

"Yeah. But forget her. Let me tell you what happened with Styro gettin' whacked. That shit was *too* crazy, on Cup."

"I read about it on Facebook. They say he got whacked on 16th."

"That nigga told on Jah about that Jamal situation. Them two racist-ass police in that black Challenger slid down on him yesterday morning and I guess they asked him about the Jamal situation. The nigga got scared and told them what he knew. The pigs stopped and told Lil Mark about it before they drove off. Lil Mark and Ceno heard the shit."

"That was some underhanded shit the law pulled," Juice said, lighting a Newport cigarette. "I wouldn't have believed it."

"That's what I said at first. But Styro was with some lil chick and she told Lil Mark she heard the nigga say the shit."

"Damn."

"I was driving down 16th last night," Wayno said, "and tell me why I see the nigga Styro hadslid off the fuckin' road. I had Lil Mark in the back with that AR on his lap. You already know how that went down. Drill, drill, drill."

Juice gazed disapprovingly at a dirty streak of liquid on his living room's glossy hardwood floor. Aside from that one dark smudge on the floor, the room was spotless with heavenly white walls, plush black leather furniture, and an enormous 85-inch 4K HDTV. This was his man-cave, where he drank beer and watched his Bears and his Bulls. There was a large tree in one corner, nearly hidden by the neatly wrapped gifts that were stacked up around it.

"My bad," Wayno said.

"For the dirt and melted snow on my floor?" Wayno nodded.

"Oh," Juice said. "I thought you were apologizing for giving the order to kill a mothafucka without asking me."

"You was way out in Cali."

"I wouldn't give fuck if I was in China! Call me and ask me before you make some fucked up decision like that."

"So you're saying I was wrong?"

"Hell yeah, nigga! You might not've been wrong for getting it done, but you did it in the dumbest spot you could've done it in. First, I got Jah doing that stupid ass hit right in the middle of Trumbull and now we got another dead body in the middle of 16th? What do you think the Chicago Police Department is about to do? Huh? Think they're just gonna keep scooping bodies off the ground and doing nothing about it? You better believe they're about to do some kinda sweep around this bitch and I'm not the one who's gotta be worried about going to jail. Not unless a nigga tell on me. You're the one out there running the show. If something goes wrong, that shit falls on *you*. Don't forget that."

"I know." Wayno hung his head in defeat. "You're right. I fucked up. I can admit that." He shook his lowered head and his dreadlocks swung like the ropes of a mop head.

Juice let a couple of minutes pass as he smoked and watched sports highlights while Wayno stewed in regret. Then, he looked at Wayno. "I called you over here for a reason."

"Yeah?" Wayno responded, raising his head.

"Yeah," Juice said. "I wanted to let you know that from now on you can get whole blocksfor fifteen racks apiece."

Wayno's eyes got wide. He stared at Juice, waiting for the catch.

"That's only for you," Juice said. "Well, you, Rell, and Jah. As many as you can buy. I got itall ready for you. And I'll front you whatever you buy."

"You serious?'

"Have I ever played when it came to money? I mean just what I said. I got 'em for the low. As a matter-of-fact, *you* got 'em for the low. Don't even *think* of me when you think of this shit. Just get it sold as quickly as possible. To the crackheads, the powder-heads, the dope boys. Anybody but the law. Travel across the city. Travel across the state. I got a ton of this shit and I want it gone in a month."

"Say no more," Wayno said, nodding and rubbing his hands together. He seemed just as happy to get the kilos as Juice was to give them to him. He was about the ages of Juice's twin daughters and to them he was the finest man on earth. He leaned forward, elbows in knees and eyes on Juice, all serious in the face. "You gotta tell me what went down in Cali. They say you was on the tour bus with *Bulletface*. I guess Jah posted the video on Facebook. Forget him, though. I wanna know if you got to meet *Alexus*."

A thoughtful grin crept slowly across Juice's mouth. He thought back to the fifteen ortwenty minutes he'd spent in that dark room last night. The sweetest moans of four beautiful women, one of whom was almost thirty times wealthier than Oprah Winfrey, filled his mind. He recalled the sweet scent of pussy wafting through the air, one of those pussies belonging to the eighty-billion-dollar woman who was currently the most lusted after, talked about, paparazzi hounded, and

Google searched person in the world. Did Juice regret the fact that he hadn't atleast tried to get Alexus to come over and join him and Bubbles? Abso-fucking-lutely! Was he going to tell Wayno about what had gone down in that dark dressing room inside of the Staples Center in Los Angeles last night? Abso-fucking-lutely not!

"Let's focus on this money," he said finally, stubbing his cigarette out in the Chicago Bears ashtray on his glass-top coffee table.

King Rio

~Chapter 29~

Jah was reclined in the passenger's seat of the black Cadillac Escalade his father had left them. He was snoozing; Rell was driving. They were on their way to Juice's place on Drake Avenue.

The only person on Jah's mind right now was Christina, one of the exotic dancers he'd met last night at the Deja and D-Boy concert. She was a sexy, petite Dominican girl from New York City. Her ass was fake, her titties were fake, and she could not have looked more stunning. She'd given him a lap dance and they'd exchanged numbers. While sitting on his lap, on top of the erection her lap dance had caused, she'd sent a video message to his phone that showed her lying on her side in bed with a dildo stuck in her butt-hole while she fucked her pussy with another dildo. She'd asked if she could come and visit him in Chicago sometime soon and he'd said yeah.

Back in his hotel suite, he and Tirzah had made up and made love until they'd fallen asleep. They'd done it again on the Gulfstream jet, then again when they got home. Every time Tirzah saw his dick was hard she would impale herself on it, thinking his randomly occurring erections were the direct result of his burning desire for make-up sex. In truth, the erections had come from him ruminating about the two-minute video Christina had sent him, playing it over and over in his head, substituting the fake plastic dicks with his real one.

The video was replaying in his mind when Rell shook him from his slumber. His eyes blinked open and he found Rell's smartphone resting on his chest.

"You got a phone call," Rell said.

Jah picked up the phone. "Yo," he said.

"Baby," Tirzah said, her voice coming through loud and

clear. "I need about seven thousand dollars to get myself a few things for Christmas…and a few things for you."

"Yeah, and people in hell need ice water.""Pleeeease."

"Yoooouuu got the game fucked up."

"Can I at least explain to you what I need the money for first?"

"Explain away." Jah fingered a switch that sent the back of his seat rising to a sitting position.

"Okay," Tirzah began, "Dolce and Gabbana got these new jeans out and I just have to have them. I found a Miu Miu bag that goes along perfectly with the jeans. I want these black and silver Valentino Garavani boots. Oooh, and this Louis Vuitton bag that fades from purple on one side to blue in the middle to green on the other side. That's only two thousand dollars."

"All that shit together is only two thousand dollars?""No, the Louis bag is two grand."

Jah shook his head. "You done yet?"

"Almost, almost. Okay, I want these white and green Tory Burch sneakers for me--they're only two twenty-five, don't panic--ad these Gucci loafers for you." She let out a breath. "And a watch for you."

"You just added that watch," Jah accused, chuckling."No I didn't." She chuckled too.

"Yes, the fuck you did. I ain't no goddamn retard. You added that watch so it wouldn't look like I was only getting the loafers." He patted his pockets, searching for his own smartphone. "Where in the fuck did I… put my… goddamn…" he murmured to himself.

"If you're looking for your iPhone it's right here," Tirzah said.

Jah's mouth dropped open. His eyelids ran away from each other and his eyeballs rolled around aimlessly in their sockets.

His breathing paused. He found himself praying, *God, please don't let her look at my text messages.*

Tirzah laughed. "Why'd you get so quiet?"

Then, *she* got quiet and he knew what was coming next if he didn't get her eyes unglued from the iPhone he'd so carelessly left charging on his bed table.

"I'll give you the money," he said, sounding like he was negotiating with a particularly heartless terrorist instead of talking to his wife. "Just... uh... make sure you get me that watch. I need a new watch. Was just thinking about getting a new watch. What kinda watch is it?" He was rambling and it was almost funny.

"Nuh uhhh," Tirzah said, dragging the *uhh* out, "wait a minute, nigga. Who in the fuck is C.T.? And why is this hoe sending you good morning texts and shit? Is this her in this video?"

Jah sighed. I done fucked up again, he thought. "Put my goddamn phone down," he said. "Always being nosy."

He expected her to call him a hundred disparaging names, to initiate a shouting match, or to threaten divorce and tell him he'd be sleeping at Rell and Tamera's place until Rhianna turned ugly and hell froze over. What he actually got was a confession that put all his emotions in a blender and turned it on high.

"It's cool," she said, suddenly calm. "I ain't even mad. I'm one up on your dog-ass anyway.

That's why I fucked Juice last night. Sucked his dick too. Haaa-ha. Joke's on you."

"Am I supposed to believe that?" Jah asked, but he was already speaking through clenched teeth and his nostrils were flared.

"You ain't gotta believe me. Ask Rell. He was in there with us. Backstage at the concert.

How you like them apples? Bitch!" She ended the call abruptly.

Teeth still clenched, nostrils still flared, jaw muscles flexing rapidly, Jah turned to Rell. His eyelids came close together and he thought back to last night when he'd stood up in Bulletface's dressing room and walked to the door, intending to go out and check the bathroom to see if Rell was there. He'd found Rell and Juice standing just outside of the door. The girls had arrived about a half an hour later and they'd left for the Four Seasons shortly thereafter.

He was wide awake now. Rell was pulling up behind Wayno's red Suburban; they were outside of Juice's building. He tossed the phone into Rell's lap and Rell looked at him.

"Jerk-ass nigga," Rell said.

"What happened between Juice and Tirzah last night?"

"Awww shit." Rell leaned his head head back and pressed a hand over his eyes. "Man, don't let that bullshit fuck up this money. This nigga got bricks for *fifteen.*" He looked to Jah again. "We can get *filthy* rich off this play. You hear me? *Filthy* rich."

"Just tell me what went down." Jah's expression was indecipherable, but on the inside he was seething. He had on a thick Moncler winter jacket, black and gold to match his Air Forces. A 30-round clip stood in the inside pocket of his jacket. It went to the Ruger pistol on his left hip.

"I really can't say exactly what went down," Rell said. "It was too dark. The light was turned off. I might've heard her moaning and what not, but--"

"*Might've*? You *might've* heard her moaning?"

"Okay, I heard it. Does it really even matter? You cheated on her with a bitch and she turned around and did the same shit with the big homie. So what? M-O-B, nigga. Don't ever forget that shit." He pushed open his door and stepped out into the street just as Juice and Wayno came walking out of the building, each of them carrying a cardboard box.

Jah pushed the 30-round magazine into his Ruger and put the gun back on his hip before he climbed out of the SUV and started off toward Juice and Wayno, who were now carefully descending the slick concrete stairs. Jah was going to kill both of them. He has his mind madeup. He would shoot Juice right in the front of that bald head and Wayno would get it next just for being with Juice at the wrong time. Jah was approaching the gate, two seconds away from drawing the Ruger and squeezing the trigger, when something in the corner of his eye caught his attention.

A black pickup truck had just slid to a stop in the middle of Drake Avenue. It was a Dodge Ram 1500, Jah noticed, with Indiana plates. The Ram's driver stuck a gun out of the window and started shooting. The next thing Jah knew, he was lying on the cold, icy sidewalk with blood on his chest watching Juice, Wayno, and Rell return fire as the Ram sped away.

King Rio

~Chapter 30~

Ashley Hunter floated into the foyer, a dark-haired Nigerian sprite with delicate features. She was wearing a one-piece, color-drunk silk creation by Brazilian swimwear designer Adriana Degreas, which made her look like a butterfly when she raised her arms.

She'd driven a couple of miles in her brand new red Porsche SUV from a Hollywood spa to T-Walk's 1920's Mediterranean-style house overlooking a creek and she found Mr. Walkson in the deep blue sitting room, kicked back on an oversize white leather sofa with his iPhone 7 Plus in hand. She sat down next to him, kissed him on the cheek, and, studying his royal blue Armani suit, said, "Pretty fly for a dead guy."

"Ain't I though?" He turned toward her and she kissed him on the mouth. "You're so damn fine," she said.

"You're the fine one," he replied.

She had a glass of health juice, prepared by the in-house raw-vegan chef she'd hired to work alongside T-Walk's carnivorous personal chef, and he had freshly squeezed orange juice. Ema, the nanny, came in with their one-year-old, T.W. (Trintino Walkson Jr.) and December, Ashley's frantically friendly Maltipoo dog.

Ashley pulled T.W. up onto her lap to keep December from repeatedly knocking him over. Her eyes went to T-Walk's phone. He was thumbing through his new Instagram page, which had already racked up over three million followers since its debut three days ago.

"Blake and Alexus tried to ruin you," Ashley said. "It's not fair that they get to live comfortably while you have to start over from scratch. Do you see how the media's babying her? If anybody else would have blasted a gun at their husband they'd have been labeled a monster. But noooo, not Alexus. They're making it out like she's the victim. She posts a pic showing her and the girls from that controversial picture Blake posted on his page and now everybody's all 'yasss, I am so here for Queen A, girl power' and all that b.s. Then, she went onstage with Blake at the Deja and D-Boy concert last night and *Blake* actually apologized to *her*. Talking about it was his fault for all the cheating he did in the past. I almost threw my damn phone when I saw that video on *The Shade Room.*"

"Did you see what they posted before that?" T-Walk asked. "That a lot of people are saying she only shot at him to get him to leave her so I can slip back into her bed?" "Yeah, I saw that b.s."

"And if you noticed, the picture she posted with those girls was taken inside that restaurant we followed the paps to last night."

"And?"

He went to his iPhone's photo gallery and pulled up a photo of him hugging Alexus at the head of a dining table. The three girls from Blake's photo were seated around the table alongwith celebrity attorney Britney Bostic.

"I had one of the bodyguards snap this pic for me," T-Walk said, handing over the phone to Ashley. "Why don't you send that to *The Shade Room?* See if we can get Blake all riled up. See if we can get him to pull a gun and send a few shots at her for a change."

"I like your brain," Ashley said, smiling broadly. "Let the petty games begin."

To Be Continued...
The Brick Man 4
Coming Soon

Lock Down Publications and Ca$h Presents assisted
publishing packages.

BASIC PACKAGE $499
Editing
Cover Design
Formatting

UPGRADED PACKAGE $800
Typing
Editing
Cover Design
Formatting

ADVANCE PACKAGE $1,200
Typing
Editing
Cover Design
Formatting
Copyright registration
Proofreading
Upload book to Amazon

LDP SUPREME PACKAGE $1,500
Typing
Editing
Cover Design
Formatting
Copyright registration
Proofreading
Set up Amazon account
Upload book to Amazon
Advertise on LDP Amazon and Facebook page

***Other services available upon request. Additional charges may apply
Lock Down Publications
P.O. Box 944
Stockbridge, GA 30281-9998
Phone # 470 303-9761

Submission Guideline

Submit the first three chapters of your completed manuscript to ldpsubmissions@gmail.com, subject line: Your book's title. The manuscript must be in a .doc file and sent as an attachment. Document should be in Times New Roman, double spaced and in size 12 font. Also, provide your synopsis and full contact information. If sending multiple submissions, they must each be in a separate email.

Have a story but no way to send it electronically? You can still submit to LDP/Ca$h Presents. Send in the first three chapters, written or typed, of your completed manuscript to:

LDP: Submissions Dept
Po Box 944
Stockbridge, Ga 30281

DO NOT send original manuscript. Must be a duplicate.

Provide your synopsis and a cover letter containing your full contact information.

Thanks for considering LDP and Ca$h Presents.

NEW RELEASES

CONFESSIONS OF A JACKBOY II by NICHO-
LAS LOCK
A GANGSTA'S KARMA 2 by FLAME
GRIMEY WAYS by RAY VINCI
A GANGSTA SAVED XMAS by MONET DRA-
GUN
XMAS WITH AN ATL SHOOTER by CA$H &
DESTINY SKAI
CUM FOR ME by SUGAR E. WALLZ
THE BRICK MAN 3 by KING RIO

Coming Soon from Lock Down Publications/Ca$h Presents

BLOOD OF A BOSS **VI**

SHADOWS OF THE GAME II

TRAP BASTARD II

By **Askari**

LOYAL TO THE GAME **IV**

By **T.J. & Jelissa**

IF TRUE SAVAGE **VIII**

MIDNIGHT CARTEL IV

DOPE BOY MAGIC IV

CITY OF KINGZ III

NIGHTMARE ON SILENT AVE II

By **Chris Green**

BLAST FOR ME **III**

A SAVAGE DOPEBOY III

CUTTHROAT MAFIA III

DUFFLE BAG CARTEL VII

HEARTLESS GOON VI

By **Ghost**

A HUSTLER'S DECEIT III

KILL ZONE II

BAE BELONGS TO ME III

By **Aryanna**

KING OF THE TRAP III

By **T.J. Edwards**

GORILLAZ IN THE BAY V

3X KRAZY III

STRAIGHT BEAST MODE II

De'Kari

KINGPIN KILLAZ IV

STREET KINGS III

PAID IN BLOOD III

CARTEL KILLAZ IV

DOPE GODS III

Hood Rich

SINS OF A HUSTLA II

ASAD

RICH $AVAGE II

MONEY IN THE GRAVE II

By Martell Troublesome Bolden

YAYO V

Bred In The Game 2

S. Allen

CREAM III

By Yolanda Moore

SON OF A DOPE FIEND III

HEAVEN GOT A GHETTO II

By Renta

LOYALTY AIN'T PROMISED III

By Keith Williams

I'M NOTHING WITHOUT HIS LOVE II

SINS OF A THUG II

TO THE THUG I LOVED BEFORE II

By Monet Dragun

The Brick Man 3

QUIET MONEY IV

EXTENDED CLIP III

THUG LIFE IV

By **Trai'Quan**

THE STREETS MADE ME IV

By **Larry D. Wright**

IF YOU CROSS ME ONCE II

By **Anthony Fields**

THE STREETS WILL NEVER CLOSE II

By **K'ajji**

HARD AND RUTHLESS III

THE BILLIONAIRE BENTLEYS II

Von Diesel

KILLA KOUNTY II

By **Khufu**

MONEY GAME III

By **Smoove Dolla**

JACK BOYZ VERSUS DOPE BOYZ

By **Romell Tukes**

MURDA WAS THE CASE II

Elijah R. Freeman

THE STREETS NEVER LET GO II

By **Robert Baptiste**

AN UNFORESEEN LOVE III

By **Meesha**

KING OF THE TRENCHES II

by **GHOST & TRANAY ADAMS**

King Rio

MONEY MAFIA II

LOYAL TO THE SOIL II

By **Jibril Williams**

QUEEN OF THE ZOO II

By **Black Migo**

THE BRICK MAN IV

By King Rio

VICIOUS LOYALTY II

By Kingpen

A GANGSTA'S PAIN II

By J-Blunt

CONFESSIONS OF A JACKBOY III

By Nicholas Lock

GRIMEY WAYS II

By Ray Vinci

Available Now

RESTRAINING ORDER **I & II**

By **CA$H & Coffee**

LOVE KNOWS NO BOUNDARIES **I II & III**

By **Coffee**

RAISED AS A GOON I, II, III & IV

BRED BY THE SLUMS I, II, III

BLAST FOR ME I & II

ROTTEN TO THE CORE I II III

A BRONX TALE I, II, III

DUFFLE BAG CARTEL I II III IV V VI

HEARTLESS GOON I II III IV V

A SAVAGE DOPEBOY I II

DRUG LORDS I II III

CUTTHROAT MAFIA I II

KING OF THE TRENCHES

By **Ghost**

LAY IT DOWN **I & II**

LAST OF A DYING BREED I II

BLOOD STAINS OF A SHOTTA I & II III

By **Jamaica**

LOYAL TO THE GAME I II III

LIFE OF SIN I, II III

By **TJ & Jelissa**

BLOODY COMMAS I & II

SKI MASK CARTEL I II & III

KING OF NEW YORK I II,III IV V

RISE TO POWER I II III

COKE KINGS I II III IV V

BORN HEARTLESS I II III IV

KING OF THE TRAP I II

By **T.J. Edwards**

IF LOVING HIM IS WRONG…I & II

LOVE ME EVEN WHEN IT HURTS I II III

By **Jelissa**

King Rio

WHEN THE STREETS CLAP BACK I & II III

THE HEART OF A SAVAGE I II III

MONEY MAFIA

LOYAL TO THE SOIL

By **Jibril Williams**

A DISTINGUISHED THUG STOLE MY HEART I II & III

LOVE SHOULDN'T HURT I II III IV

RENEGADE BOYS I II III IV

PAID IN KARMA I II III

SAVAGE STORMS I II

AN UNFORESEEN LOVE I II

By **Meesha**

A GANGSTER'S CODE I &, II III

A GANGSTER'S SYN I II III

THE SAVAGE LIFE I II III

CHAINED TO THE STREETS I II III

BLOOD ON THE MONEY I II III

A GANGSTA'S PAIN

By **J-Blunt**

PUSH IT TO THE LIMIT

By **Bre' Hayes**

BLOOD OF A BOSS **I, II, III, IV, V**

SHADOWS OF THE GAME

TRAP BASTARD

By **Askari**

THE STREETS BLEED MURDER **I, II & III**

THE HEART OF A GANGSTA I II& III

202

The Brick Man 3

By **Jerry Jackson**

CUM FOR ME I II III IV V VI VII VIII

An **LDP Erotica Collaboration**

BRIDE OF A HUSTLA **I II & II**

THE FETTI GIRLS **I, II& III**

CORRUPTED BY A GANGSTA I, II III, IV

BLINDED BY HIS LOVE

THE PRICE YOU PAY FOR LOVE I, II ,III

DOPE GIRL MAGIC I II III

By **Destiny Skai**

WHEN A GOOD GIRL GOES BAD·

By **Adrienne**

THE COST OF LOYALTY I II III

By Kweli

A GANGSTER'S REVENGE **I II III & IV**

THE BOSS MAN'S DAUGHTERS I II III IV V

A SAVAGE LOVE **I & II**

BAE BELONGS TO ME I II

A HUSTLER'S DECEIT I, II, III

WHAT BAD BITCHES DO I, II, III

SOUL OF A MONSTER I II III

KILL ZONE

A DOPE BOY'S QUEEN I II III

By **Aryanna**

A KINGPIN'S AMBITON

A KINGPIN'S AMBITION **II**

I MURDER FOR THE DOUGH

King Rio

By **Ambitious**
TRUE SAVAGE I II III IV V VI VII
DOPE BOY MAGIC I, II, III
MIDNIGHT CARTEL I II III
CITY OF KINGZ I II
NIGHTMARE ON SILENT AVE
By **Chris Green**
A DOPEBOY'S PRAYER
By **Eddie "Wolf" Lee**
THE KING CARTEL **I, II & III**
By **Frank Gresham**
THESE NIGGAS AIN'T LOYAL **I, II & III**
By **Nikki Tee**
GANGSTA SHYT **I II &III**
By **CATO**
THE ULTIMATE BETRAYAL
By **Phoenix**
BOSS'N UP **I , II & III**
By **Royal Nicole**
I LOVE YOU TO DEATH
By **Destiny J**
I RIDE FOR MY HITTA
I STILL RIDE FOR MY HITTA
By **Misty Holt**
LOVE & CHASIN' PAPER
By **Qay Crockett**
TO DIE IN VAIN

SINS OF A HUSTLA

By **ASAD**

BROOKLYN HUSTLAZ

By **Boogsy Morina**

BROOKLYN ON LOCK I & II

By **Sonovia**

GANGSTA CITY

By **Teddy Duke**

A DRUG KING AND HIS DIAMOND I & II III

A DOPEMAN'S RICHES

HER MAN, MINE'S TOO I, II

CASH MONEY HO'S

THE WIFEY I USED TO BE I II

By Nicole Goosby

TRAPHOUSE KING **I II & III**

KINGPIN KILLAZ I II III

STREET KINGS I II

PAID IN BLOOD **I II**

CARTEL KILLAZ I II III

DOPE GODS I II

By **Hood Rich**

LIPSTICK KILLAH **I, II, III**

CRIME OF PASSION I II & III

FRIEND OR FOE I II III

By **Mimi**

STEADY MOBBN' **I, II, III**

THE STREETS STAINED MY SOUL I II

King Rio

By **Marcellus Allen**

WHO SHOT YA **I, II, III**

SON OF A DOPE FIEND I II

HEAVEN GOT A GHETTO

Renta

GORILLAZ IN THE BAY **I II III IV**

TEARS OF A GANGSTA I II

3X KRAZY I II

STRAIGHT BEAST MODE

DE'KARI

TRIGGADALE I II III

MURDAROBER WAS THE CASE

Elijah R. Freeman

GOD BLESS THE TRAPPERS I, II, III

THESE SCANDALOUS STREETS I, II, III

FEAR MY GANGSTA I, II, III IV, V

THESE STREETS DON'T LOVE NOBODY I, II

BURY ME A G I, II, III, IV, V

A GANGSTA'S EMPIRE I, II, III, IV

THE DOPEMAN'S BODYGAURD I II

THE REALEST KILLAZ I II III

THE LAST OF THE OGS I II III

Tranay Adams

THE STREETS ARE CALLING

Duquie Wilson

MARRIED TO A BOSS I II III

By Destiny Skai & Chris Green

KINGZ OF THE GAME I II III IV V VI

Playa Ray

SLAUGHTER GANG I II III

RUTHLESS HEART I II III

By Willie Slaughter

FUK SHYT

By Blakk Diamond

DON'T F#CK WITH MY HEART I II

By Linnea

ADDICTED TO THE DRAMA I II III

IN THE ARM OF HIS BOSS II

By Jamila

YAYO I II III IV

A SHOOTER'S AMBITION I II

BRED IN THE GAME

By S. Allen

TRAP GOD I II III

RICH $AVAGE

MONEY IN THE GRAVE I II

By Martell Troublesome Bolden

FOREVER GANGSTA

GLOCKS ON SATIN SHEETS I II

By Adrian Dulan

TOE TAGZ I II III

LEVELS TO THIS SHYT I II

By Ah'Million

KINGPIN DREAMS I II III

King Rio

By Paper Boi Rari
CONFESSIONS OF A GANGSTA I II III IV
CONFESSIONS OF A JACKBOY I II
By Nicholas Lock
I'M NOTHING WITHOUT HIS LOVE
SINS OF A THUG
TO THE THUG I LOVED BEFORE
A GANGSTA SAVED XMAS
By Monet Dragun
CAUGHT UP IN THE LIFE I II III
THE STREETS NEVER LET GO
By Robert Baptiste
NEW TO THE GAME I II III
MONEY, MURDER & MEMORIES I II III
By **Malik D. Rice**
LIFE OF A SAVAGE I II III
A GANGSTA'S QUR'AN I II III
MURDA SEASON I II III
GANGLAND CARTEL I II III
CHI'RAQ GANGSTAS I II III
KILLERS ON ELM STREET I II III
JACK BOYZ N DA BRONX I II III
A DOPEBOY'S DREAM I II III
By **Romell Tukes**
LOYALTY AIN'T PROMISED I II
By Keith Williams
QUIET MONEY I II III

The Brick Man 3

THUG LIFE I II III

EXTENDED CLIP I II

By **Trai'Quan**

THE STREETS MADE ME I II III

By **Larry D. Wright**

THE ULTIMATE SACRIFICE I, II, III, IV, V, VI

KHADIFI

IF YOU CROSS ME ONCE

ANGEL I II

IN THE BLINK OF AN EYE

By **Anthony Fields**

THE LIFE OF A HOOD STAR

By **Ca$h & Rashia Wilson**

THE STREETS WILL NEVER CLOSE

By **K'ajji**

CREAM I II

By **Yolanda Moore**

NIGHTMARES OF A HUSTLA I II III

By **King Dream**

CONCRETE KILLA I II

VICIOUS LOYALTY

By **Kingpen**

HARD AND RUTHLESS I II

MOB TOWN 251

THE BILLIONAIRE BENTLEYS

By **Von Diesel**

GHOST MOB

King Rio

Stilloan Robinson

MOB TIES I II III IV

By SayNoMore

BODYMORE MURDERLAND I II III

By Delmont Player

FOR THE LOVE OF A BOSS

By C. D. Blue

MOBBED UP I II III IV

THE BRICK MAN I II III

By King Rio

KILLA KOUNTY

By Khufu

MONEY GAME I II

By Smoove Dolla

A GANGSTA'S KARMA I II

By FLAME

KING OF THE TRENCHES II

by **GHOST & TRANAY ADAMS**

QUEEN OF THE ZOO

By **Black Migo**

GRIMEY WAYS

By Ray Vinci

XMAS WITH AN ATL SHOOTER

By Ca$h & Destiny Skai

BOOKS BY LDP'S CEO, CA$H

TRUST IN NO MAN

TRUST IN NO MAN 2

TRUST IN NO MAN 3

BONDED BY BLOOD

SHORTY GOT A THUG

THUGS CRY

THUGS CRY 2

THUGS CRY 3

TRUST NO BITCH

TRUST NO BITCH 2

TRUST NO BITCH 3

TIL MY CASKET DROPS

RESTRAINING ORDER

RESTRAINING ORDER 2

IN LOVE WITH A CONVICT

LIFE OF A HOOD STAR

XMAS WITH AN ATL SHOOTER

King Rio